Veil of
Anarchy

A Kessler Effect Novel: Book One

Vannetta Chapman

Contents

Dedicated to Pam Lindman
and Heather Blodgett

"We shall require a substantially new manner of thinking if mankind is to survive."
~Albert Einstein

"Rage, rage against the dying of the light."
from *Do Not Go Gentle into that Good Night*
~Dylan Thomas

"We are entering a new era of debris control...
an era that will be dominated by a slowly increasing number of random catastrophic collisions."
~Donald Kessler

"This is the way the world ends
Not with a bang but a whimper."
~T.S. Eliot

Prologue-Veil of Mystery

Alpine, Texas

The first anomaly occurred on Tuesday morning at fourteen minutes after ten. Keme Lopez noted the time, confirmed that his back-up system had taken a screenshot of all open windows, and replayed the video that had appeared on Twitter. There wasn't much to it—a mere fourteen seconds from start to finish. Already it was at the top of his Twitter feed.

He sat back, trying to understand what he'd seen. Trying to come up with a better explanation than the Twitter universe had. Slowly, cautiously—as if playing the video might cause some danger to befall him and his family—he again clicked *play*.

A woman with short blonde hair sobbed as she recorded live. He could see the *Recording Live* button at the bottom of the screen. The video definitely represented something that had happened in real time. From the looks of the people in the background, what he was seeing had actually occurred.

As tears streamed down her face and in words that were nearly incoherent, she told her husband that she loved him.

Keme paused the video.

He zoomed in on passengers in the background. Some huddled together, heads bowed, praying. A mother in the next row rocked her child back and forth. Many passengers had their hands over their faces, and about a third sat in the classic "prepare for crash" position. Several men stood, though the nose-down angle of the plane obviously made that difficult. They seemed to be looking out the window.

When Keme zoomed in more, he was able to see clear blue skies. So this plane crash—if that's what it was—was not weather-related.

Mechanical failure? But there was no smoke that he could see. No holes in the plane. It seemed to be simply falling from the sky.

A soft rap on his open door jerked him back to the present—a June morning in Alpine, Texas.

"I'm headed outside to work in the garden," Lucy said.

Keme's wife was a professor of literature at Sul Ross University. She was five foot, four inches with a curvy figure and brown hair—the tips dyed with turquoise streaks. Keme had married up, and he realized that anew every single day.

"What would make a plane fall from the sky?"

"Excuse me?"

"Mechanical failure, a bomb exploding, maybe a pilot who had a heart attack..."

"Not the last one." She moved into the room and stared at his screen, then reached past him and clicked *Play*. She watched the video in silence, then played it again. Finally, she stepped back, leaning against the doorframe and staring up at the ceiling.

He waited.

Finally her brown eyes met his.

"That's awful. Is it real?"

"Seems to be. Why did you say '*not the last one?*'"

"Because that's what a co-pilot rides along for, and I think...I think a plane switches to automatic pilot if something unusual happens."

"Probably so."

"When was that video recorded?"

Keme glanced at the time on his computer. "Almost fifteen minutes ago."

"Anything on the news sites?"

He clicked to a different tab and unmuted the window.

"The video was apparently taken aboard a direct flight from London to Austin just a few minutes ago. According to the FAA—"

The screen abruptly went to a plain blue background with *Please Stand By* displayed in a large font. Beneath it was a banner which read *We are experiencing technical problems at this time.*

"What happened?"

"I don't know." He again noted the time—10:30. "They've just stopped streaming."

He clicked over to two other news stations, but they both displayed the same blue screen with the same disclaimer.

"Is the internet down?"

"Doesn't seem to be." He clicked back to Twitter.

Top story—#Planecrash

Second story--#newsoutage

"An EMP?" Lucy crossed her arms, frowning at the screen.

"The internet is still up. I guess it could be a localized EMP, but the odds that it would affect all news outlets seems...impossible."

Lucy squeezed his shoulder, then kissed his cheek. "Let me know if anything else bizarre happens."

"Where are you going?"

"To weed the garden."

Which was exactly like Lucy. She was somewhat unflappable. A nuclear bomb could be headed their way, and she'd say, "I certainly can't stop a nuke. Might as well weed the garden." She was very big on ignoring things out of her scope of influence. Maybe not ignoring, but she certainly didn't spend hours worrying over it. He envied her that, even as he watched her walk away.

His eyes scanned the shelves in his office which held a wide variety of items that he thought of as simply—*my history*. There were water sticks, deer antlers, arrow heads, and rocks. The collection represented his Native American heritage. His mother was one quarter Kiowa. His father was Hispanic, and it was from his father that he'd inherited his handiness. For his Pop that meant farm equipment. For Keme, it meant computers.

A long workspace counter stretched along two walls of his office, and it was filled with computers. At the age of forty-two, he managed to make a pretty good living fixing people's computers. Alpine was only six thousand folks. Given their remote location in the southwest corner of Texas, computers were how they remained connected to the rest of the world.

He turned his attention back to his monitor.

For the next twenty minutes he browsed the world wide web, but there was no consensus as to what had happened. Definitely no official statement.

Then he clicked back to Twitter and saw that the plane crash had been bumped down to the number two spot. In its place was the hashtag #stockmarketcollapse.

Keme no longer invested his money in the stock market, but he did stay apprised of the general situation. There'd been a lot of "collapses" in the last few years. It usually meant the market dropped ten percent then rebounded twelve to fifteen percent the next day. He was pretty sure the market was manipulated so that the ups and downs made the rich richer and kept everyone not in that group out.

Just another of your conspiracy theories, Lucy was fond of saying.

He clicked on #stockmarketcollapse and scanned through the posts.

As he watched, the ticker went from a seventy-five percent loss to an eighty percent loss.

The DOW had dropped eighty percent? That wasn't possible. Circuit breaker rules had been put in place in 1988 to protect companies against panic selling. He tried clicking over to another site, but now his machine seemed frozen. None of the sites would refresh. He leaned back in his chair to check his modem. Red lights blinked back at him.

It wasn't unusual for the internet to go down in Alpine. They were, after all, in a rural part of Texas. Keme picked up his cellphone and stared at the icon in the upper right. No internet signal at all. Furthermore, when he tried to place a call, it wouldn't connect.

So the internet was down, as well as the cell towers?

Pocketing the device, he grabbed his hat and stepped outside.

Lucy was squatting in front of the tomato plants. Sitting back on her heels, she asked, "Any answers?"

"Nope."

"More questions?"

"Yup. Internet is out completely and so are the phones."

"Huh."

Keme glanced north toward Alpine. "The stock market crashed just before the internet went down."

"By how much?"

"Eighty percent."

Lucy wiped away sweat from her brow. "I didn't think that was possible."

"It shouldn't be."

She stood and brushed at the dirt on the back of her jeans. Walking over to him, she cocked her head and studied him. "You're worried."

He shrugged, then admitted, "Yeah."

"Akule is fine, honey. She's right there..." Lucy jerked a thumb toward Alpine. "We can go check on her if you like."

Their daughter had recently moved back to Alpine, but their son, Paco, lived with his wife and children in the Dallas area. If something big was happening, Keme would like to have his family close.

"Have you called Tanda?"

He smiled, kissed her forehead, and pulled her into his arms. "Phones are out. Remember?"

"Oh, yeah." She snuggled against him. "Sounds like you won't be fixing anyone's computer this morning. How about you and I go inside and—"

At that moment there was an explosion that caused the ground to tremble.

"What—"

"Look."

A cloud of smoke was rising on the horizon. Something had exploded. The scream of emergency vehicles immediately followed. Whatever was happening, it was happening in the middle of Alpine.

They both jogged back inside. Keme grabbed his wallet and keys. Lucy snatched up her purse and her phone, then dropped the phone inside her bag with a shake of her head.

"Let's go," he said.

Though they lived only a few miles outside of town, a traffic jam had formed on TX-118 slowing their progress. Keme finally turned off and drove along a back road, wound his way toward the downtown area, and stopped a few blocks shy of the main business area.

"Should we head to the police station?" Lucy's eyes were wide, but she wasn't panicking. Her voice was steady. She was analyzing instead of just reacting.

Keme suspected she was trying to put together what was happening in front of their eyes with what he'd shown her on the computer. But how could those things possibly be connected?

"You go to Akule's," he said. "I'll go to the police station."

"Meet back here?"

"No. Do you have any cash?"

She pulled out her billfold and thumbed through it. "About sixty dollars."

"Okay." He gave her five more twenty-dollar bills from his wallet. He gave her everything he had. "We still have the emergency money at home, right?"

"Yeah. Five hundred."

"Good. Then let's meet at the Grocery Mart. If you get there before me, load up with canned goods. Nothing perishable."

"You want me to spend a hundred and sixty dollars on canned food?"

"Yeah." He kissed her forehead. "Shop like it's your last time, because something tells me it may be."

He jogged toward the police station, but even as he walked through the door, he knew he wouldn't find his sister. No way the chief of police would be sitting at her desk while something burned in downtown Alpine.

"She's not here," Edna said.

Edna was the receptionist, but Keme knew from what Tanda often said that she was a whole lot more. In her mid-fifties, Edna kept the police station working smoothly and efficiently. Tanda had gone as far as to joke that if Edna ever quit, she was going to hand in her badge and take up fishing for a living.

"What's going on?"

"Train crash."

"Wow."

"Yeah. Rattled our window panes. Must have been a bad one. We have officers at the location, helping with casualties."

"Okay. Should I go over there?"

"I'm sure emergency personnel have it under control. Fire department will be there as well. As loud as that collision was, I have a feeling that agents from the Federal Railroad Agency will be here before dark."

Keme wasn't so sure, but it probably wasn't the best time to share his theories with her. That's all they were at this point—theories.

"I'd raise her on the radio for you, but somehow...don't ask me how because I'm not as tech savvy as you are, Keme Lopez, but somehow that train crash has caused our comm units to go out."

Only that wasn't possible because Keme's phone had gone out before the train crash.

"Lights are still working," he pointed out.

"For now."

"Leave her a note that I came by?"

"Of course."

"And tell her I'll check on Akule as well as Mom and Pop."

"Will do."

He walked out of the station and looked right and left. Although the traffic continued to be backed up, there wasn't exactly any evidence of panic among the citizens of Alpine. As he made his way toward the Grocery Mart he noticed a few people lined up at the ATM machine. The signal lights blinked red, and several teenagers walked around with their cell phones held high over their heads, as if another six inches would allow them to catch a signal.

He ducked into the pharmacy, grabbed one of the hand baskets, and loaded up on emergency supplies—anesthetic spray, gauze pads, adhesive bandages, antihistamine cream, latex gloves, antidiarrheal medicine, aspirin, cough medicine, ibuprofen, moleskin, and oral decongestant.

Jack, the pharmacist, stared at the full basket in surprise. Jack was highly regarded in Alpine. He was short with glasses and wispy blonde hair. He seemed ageless. Jack had always been there, taking care of the folks of Alpine. Looking at Keme's purchases, he shrugged and said, "Credit card machine is down. Got any cash?"

"Just gave it all to Lucy."

Jack smiled and began ringing up his purchases. "I have your credit card number on file. I'll put it through when the lines are up again."

"Thanks." Keme felt a little bad about that. He didn't think the lines would be up anytime soon. On the other hand, the stuff he'd dropped into the basket could be critical supplies.

"You know you can buy all this stuff in an emergency kit."

"Do you sell those?"

"Sure." Jack pointed to a shelf in the back corner.

Keme walked over, chose the largest, and added it to the stack of goods on the counter.

"You want the kit and..."

"Yeah."

"What's going on, Keme?"

"I really don't know."

"But you think something is going on."

Keme pulled in a deep breath. He didn't know Jack well, but they'd been on a first name basis for quite a few years. He remembered that Jack had a wife and three teenagers.

"I think something has happened...something beyond Alpine."

"Like?"

"I don't know. But the phone service and the internet went down before the train accident, not after it."

"Huh."

"And before that, the stock market crashed by eighty percent."

Jack stopped ringing things up and peered at Keme over the tops of his glasses. "You mean eight percent."

"I mean eighty, and yeah...the circuit breakers should have prevented that from happening. They didn't. So something is happening."

Jack didn't respond right away. He bagged up Keme's supplies and had him sign a receipt for the total.

"I have cash at home, Ray. If the internet doesn't come back up, I'll come by and pay you."

"Okay."

"But I suggest you switch to a cash-only policy for the duration."

Jack nodded once, his expression giving away very little.

Keme had reached the door when he called out, "Be careful."

"Yeah. You too."

Keme found Lucy in the canned vegetable aisle. The bottom of the cart was filled with cans of tuna and chicken.

"What did Tanda say?"

"She wasn't there. How was Akule?"

"Also wasn't home. I left a note."

"Okay."

Lucy put both hands on her hips, still staring at the green beans. She finally looked up at Keme. "What am I doing here? Buying for the apocalypse?"

He stepped closer and lowered his voice. "Edna thinks that the crash caused the phones to go out, but we know it happened the other way around."

"I don't understand what that means."

"We saw the video footage of the plane going down, saw the news stations abruptly going off-line, and we saw the reports of the stock market crash."

Lucy reached for a can of green beans, but Keme stayed her hand. "The canned meat was smart. We'll need powdered milk, packages of beans—not cans, sugar, flour, salt." He stopped because he was trying to envision the list he'd created several years earlier during the pandemic, when they weren't sure if or when the next shipment of food would come into Alpine.

"Is this another one of your conspiracy theories?"

"It's only a theory if it isn't true. These events are connected, Lucy. They have to be." He snapped his fingers. "Bags of rice, honey, peanut butter, crackers, cornbread..."

Seeing the flustered look on her face, he said, "Give me your phone."

"But it doesn't work."

He held out his hand. Lucy rolled her eyes, dug the phone from her bag, and passed it to him. He opened up the Notes app and typed in the list, adding coffee, oats, pasta.

"Do we have a can opener?"

"Of course we have a can opener. How do you think..."

"Electric?"

"Yes." Realization was dawning in Lucy's eyes.

A few more people had come into the store, but it didn't look as if anyone else was panic buying yet. They would. When they realized their ATM and credit cards weren't working, when they understood that Alpine might not see another food delivery for some time...then the panic buying would start in earnest.

"Buy a hand operated one. Think old school."

"Where are you going?"

"To get the truck."

Keme and Lucy stopped by his parents' place on the way home. Lucy's parents had passed a few years earlier, but Keme's lived just outside of town. They, too, had heard the train crash. Keme suspected everyone in Brewster County had heard it. They knew nothing about the internet being down or the stock market crash.

"How are you doing on food?"

"Just bought groceries yesterday," his mother assured him.

"And medicine?"

"Medicine?"

"Yeah. How much of Abuela's insulin do you have?"

"I bought it yesterday too. Keme, you're scaring me. What is this about?"

His father walked in at that moment. Keme looked to Lucy, who nodded once. "We better sit down."

He told them what he knew, then what he suspected.

"I don't know, son." His father glanced at his mother, then back at him. "You could be right. Or you could be wrong."

"Yes, but what's the harm in being prepared?"

"None, I suppose. We're as prepared as we can be out here though."

"Fill your tubs with water. Even though you're on well water, you're dependent on the electric pump. If the electricity goes out, so will the pump. Also fill any containers you have."

"Good idea," his father agreed.

"And Pop..." He knew how this was going to sound, but there was just no way around it. "Make sure you have plenty of ammo."

"Ammo?"

"Yeah. Just in case."

"For the rifle or the handgun?"

"Both."

His abuela had been sitting in her rocker in the other room. Keme was never sure how much she heard or how much she understood. She would turn ninety in a few months. She seemed to have shrunk to the size of a bird, but there was still a sparkle in her eyes.

"You are a good boy to check on your parents, Keme."

He squatted by her chair. "No one else calls me a boy, Abuela."

She patted his cheek, then leaned forward and kissed his forehead. It made Keme feel young again, and for just a moment the knots that had been forming in the muscles along his shoulders eased. He patted her hand and stood.

"I'll be back to check on you, at least once a week."

"Do you think it will last that long?" his mother asked.

"Yeah. I do."

Keme and Lucy rode back to their home in silence. They'd visited his parents. They'd purchased supplies. Lucy had left a note for Akule. Which only left their son...

"I know you're worried about Pablo," he said, reaching for Lucy's hand.

"Yes and no. He's a smart young man. He'll do whatever has to be done, but..."

"But you wish he were closer."

"Yeah. I do."

As they walked into their home, a double-wide trailer that they'd purchased when their children were young, Keme found himself grateful for a good many things.

His wife was steady, slow to panic, a real port in a storm.

His parents remained quite self-sufficient.

Akule was back in Alpine and not bouncing around Austin.

And Pablo, though he was far away, was with his own family. He was where he should be. He was with his son and daughter. Pablo would react well in a crisis, and if need be, he would get his family out of the metroplex and come home.

As Keme carried bags of canned goods from the truck into the trailer, his eyes fell on what had once been their liquor cabinet. He closed his eyes, remembered the smell of it, the taste on his tongue...but mostly he remembered the regret that followed each night of drinking.

Lucy had her head deep in the pantry. She called out, "Where are we going to put all of this?"

"We could use the liquor cabinet."

Lucy set down the cans of tuna she had been trying to fit on the shelf, walked over to him, and stood on tiptoe to kiss his lips. "Indeed, we can," she said, and then they walked back outside to retrieve more of the groceries.

They spent the next few hours preparing as best they could. Both tubs and every container they could find were filled with water. Keme checked the ammunition for his handgun and his hunting rifle. He thought he had a sufficient supply for the handgun, but the hunting rifle might soon be providing their meals.

He needed to head back to town. He pulled cash from their emergency stash and told Lucy what he was about to do.

She said, "I'll ride along. I'd really like to check on my students."

"Thought you were on summer break."

It was a running joke between them. Lucy looked forward to summer break throughout the nine-month academic year, but when it came, she invariably had trouble stepping away from the college campus and her students. She was like a mother hen in that way.

Things hadn't changed much in town. There were still more cars than usual. Quite a few were parked outside the police station. There was also a line stretching around the block at the ATM machine. Keme didn't stop. They would get by with what money they had. If things were as bad as he suspected, money would cease to matter very quickly. And if things weren't as bad as he suspected, then the little he and Lucy had been able to save was safe in the bank.

The bank.

"What happens when that machine runs out of money?" Lucy asked, mirroring his thoughts.

"Things get ugly."

"But...the bank will open, right? I mean, it's after five now, but it'll be open tomorrow?"

"I don't know, Lucy." At the look of concern on her face, he added, "Small banks have no cash reserve requirement."

"What?"

"But, of course, they do keep cash on hand. Three percent is the general rule."

"Three percent? So if we had $10,000 in our savings..."

"Which we don't."

"They'd only have three hundred of that in the bank?"

"Look at it this way. People put money in a bank, the bank loans the money to someone else."

"But what if I want my money? On a normal day, I mean."

"Then you withdraw it. Remember, there's three percent of everyone's money in there."

"Okay."

"The problem comes when everyone tries to withdraw all of their funds at the same time."

Keme wasn't sure that banks would survive a complete grid collapse, and he was beginning to think that was what they were facing. Did banking institutions keep paper back-up files of loans and balances? Doubtful. Physical currency accounted for somewhere between eight and eleven percent of the Gross Domestic Product of the USA monetary system. The rest was comprised of digital deposits, crypto-currency, etc. When there was no record of those things, their value was basically wiped away. At least, he thought that was how it would work.

Keme had always been fascinated by the growing dependence on technology in general and digital wealth in particular. He'd actually tried attending Sul Ross for a business degree, but he'd found that his temperament didn't sync with formal education. When a topic interested him, he would follow the information trail as far as he could. Then he'd dig a little further.

He respected the old ways of his ancestors, and he was fascinated by people's dependence on the digital structure that had been built around society.

Most people had no idea how to hunt for their dinner.

Many people had never grown a garden.

It wasn't just that they, as a society, had grown soft. It was that they'd lost the ability to conceive of life without the benefits of internet shopping, digital banking, and virtual meetings. Folks in rural areas would be better prepared than people in large urban areas, but not by much. As a society, they had simply allowed themselves to be lulled to sleep by the ease and convenience of modern living.

He dropped Lucy off in front of the Administration Building on the Sul Ross campus. The campus was on a hill and provided an excellent view of the surrounding area. Keme paused at the end of the drive, scanning the horizon, but there was nothing that reflected what he thought was happening.

The Chihuahuan desert spread out in the distance, and beyond that he could see the Davis Mountains to the north. To the south lay the Chisos Mountains and the Mexican border. For better or worse, they were an isolated oasis in the midst of miles and miles of undeveloped land.

He drove to the gun shop and parked in front, surprised to see no other cars there.

Walking inside, he said hello to Jeannie, who was working behind the counter, found the shells he needed for his rifle, and picked up a half a dozen boxes.

Jeannie raised an eyebrow, but simply waited to see what else he would purchase. He decided on two more boxes for the handgun. He set it all on the counter.

Jeanie was maybe fifty years old, maybe sixty. It was difficult to tell. Her skin was wrinkled and leathery. She wore no make-up, and her fingers were stained from nicotine.

"I'm surprised you're not busier."

"Why would we be?"

She pulled out a pad of paper and began writing down his purchases.

"You know...the train crash, the internet being down, all of that."

Jeannie grunted. After she'd totaled the purchased, she spun the pad around so that he could see it. He counted out the bills and waited for his change.

"You think this is the big one, Keme?"

"I don't know. Maybe."

"We have two kinds of customers here. The ones who are what those television shows call survivalists. Now, I never liked that term because it seems that we're all just trying to survive. But I understand what they mean, and you do too. That's why you're here."

Keme nodded and waited.

It was plain that Jeannie wasn't done.

"Then there's your urban cowboys. I say cowboys, but the term encompasses women, men, even young folks. They like the *idea* of being prepared, but they don't have the imagination to actually envision it being necessary. They're the people who come in and buy all my shooting targets. Oh, they might hunt once or twice a year, but if they shoot a buck, they'll have someone else field-dress it."

"Okay." Something about sparring with Jeannie felt good, felt normal. He'd had similar conversations with her before. "So you're saying that your serious customers don't need to pop in for extra ammo."

"Correct."

"And your urban cowboys don't even realize they might need it."

"Also correct."

"So where am I in this scenario?"

"You, my friend, are bridging two worlds, as you've always done."

Keme sat in his truck a few minutes, trying to think of where else he needed to go, what else he needed to do. Maybe he was too tired. Maybe his brain had slipped into overdrive. He couldn't think of a single thing that would help prepare them for the next day or the day after that, and he didn't want to eat into any more of his money reserve. He still needed to go back and pay Jack, but that would wait for another day.

So instead he headed over to Sul Ross to pick up his wife.

"How were your students?"

"Confused." Lucy swiped blue strands of hair out of her face. She'd dyed it just before the students broke for summer break. She said it made her feel young and free.

He kissed her, then jammed the truck into drive.

"Let's see if Akule's home."

Their daughter had bounced around for a time after graduating from Alpine High School. She'd finally come home, taken a job as a waitress at the local steak house, and moved in with two friends. Keme thought their youngest was a bit lost, but Lucy said it wasn't unusual for her age. Since his wife knew more about kids today than he did, Keme had decided to take her word for it.

They found Akule sitting outside her apartment, staring down at the blank screen on her phone. She popped up out of the chair and gave both Lucy and Keme a hug, something she'd stopped doing in the last year. At least something good had come of this tragedy.

Akule had some of Keme's height. She was a good two inches taller than her mom, had dark brown eyes, a thin build, and beautiful black hair that she'd recently had chopped by someone who could not have known what they were doing. Or maybe she'd done it herself.

"All the phones are out," Akule said.

"Correct."

"Why doesn't our television work?"

"Streaming services depend on internet."

"Right..." She pushed her phone into her back pocket and motioned toward the two chairs. "You guys sit. Explain this to me, because I can't...I can't get hold of anyone."

Keme shared what they knew, what they'd seen so far, and what he'd witnessed on his computer before the internet had shut off.

"I don't know what any of that means."

"Neither do we," Lucy said. "It'll be okay. We're here, together, and it'll be okay."

"I wish Paco was here."

"Paco can take care of himself." Keme sat forward in the chair, elbows braced on his knees. "Do you want to come home?"

"No. I mean, if I decide to then I'll drive over, but for now I'm fine." She hesitated, then offered her first smile of the afternoon. "GPS is out. Did you know that? Good thing you taught me how to read a map."

"And change a tire."

Akule rolled her eyes. "It's like all those stupid movies I used to watch. Like end of the world, apocalypse shit."

Lucy didn't call her on the language. Lucy had tried to raise their children to have a full and rich vocabulary, but sometimes you had to call a thing what it was. Keme thought *apocalypse shit* covered it pretty well.

They spent a few more minutes reassuring her, reminded her there was plenty of room if she decided to come home, and then all three walked back to Keme's truck.

"We checked on your grandparents. They're fine."

"And Abuela?"

"She doesn't understand what we're worried about."

They all smiled at that. Abuela had her own view of the world, and there was no convincing her to see it otherwise.

"What about Tanda?"

"I stopped by, but she wasn't there. With the train crash, I imagine she's going to be busy for a day or so."

Akule gave them one final hug, then walked back to her apartment and flopped down into her chair.

"I wish she'd come home," Keme said.

Lucy simply patted his hand.

They had a simple dinner of sandwiches and chips, and though they'd never been one to have the TV running for background noise, the evening seemed eerily quiet. The power had been blinking on and off throughout the late afternoon. At sunset, as was their custom, they sat out on the porch steps, watching the sun drop below the horizon. Watching the last rays of light spread across the Chihuahuan desert.

Would they remember this night forever?

Or would they, in a week or so, look back on it and laugh at their worries?

Lucy sat on a step below his and leaned against his legs. "Do you think this is it?"

"Depends."

"On?"

"On whether you want the truth or you want me to make you feel better."

She turned around and gave him *the look*. It made him laugh. She made him laugh, even during this. He held up his hands in mock surrender. Lucy had never been the type of woman who wanted to be placated. She always wanted the truth, no matter how much it might hurt her.

"My instincts tell me that this could be the bad one."

She nodded, but she didn't speak for a moment. When she finally did, her words were not what he expected.

"There's a reason I chose poetry for my graduate level emphasis. I like the economy of words. I like how it only allows space for the essential."

An owl called out.

Crickets sang.

Wind rustled the leaves of the trees.

"If this is that...if this is our life sifted down to its most essential, then I'm glad I'm here with you."

Instead of answering, he kissed the top of her head.

They didn't talk about what they'd miss the most or how they'd survive. Those things would wait for another day. As night fell across the land, Keme wrapped his arms around his wife and thanked a god that he hadn't spoken to in quite some time that they were together.

After another half hour, they went inside and made love, then he held Lucy in his arms until her breathing evened out and he was sure she was asleep. When he was certain he wouldn't wake her, he inched from the bed and walked to the kitchen.

He sat at the table in the dark, cradling a cold cup of coffee. As the hands on the clock inched toward dawn, he tossed around everything he knew, everything he thought he knew, and how those things could be connected. He came up with three possible scenarios. None of them were good.

"How late were you up?"

"Pretty late."

"Did you sleep at all?"

"Not really." When the sky lightened before dawn, Keme had gone out to their shed and found their old camping stove. He'd opened all the windows in the kitchen, set the cookstove up on the counter, filled a kettle with water, and set it to boil when he'd heard Lucy stirring.

"Ummm. Campground coffee."

"Better than that—we have instant. Or tea."

"I'll take the instant."

She didn't speak for a moment, and he knew that she was piecing together all that had happened the day before, and trying to anticipate what would happen next.

She finally sighed and said, "Cooking is going to be interesting."

"We should eat what's in the fridge first. Lights will probably come back on, but I don't think it will last. I suspect they'll be out completely soon."

Instead of answering, she stood, walked to the refrigerator, and pulled out the jug of milk. He grabbed two boxes of cereal, two spoons, and two bowls. They ate in silence. Finally, she pushed the bowl away and said, "Might as well tell me what you're thinking."

"Okay. I can come up with three possibilities."

"Am I going to like any of them?"

"Probably not."

Lucy smiled and motioned for him to continue.

"Domestic terrorism—"

"An attack from someone within our country, against our infrastructure..." Lucy shook her head. "They'd be as affected by it as we are. What would be the point?"

"Well, they might be better prepared. Or they might be nihilists."

"Tell me you have a better theory because that one is too depressing to consider this early in the morning."

"International terrorism."

"An attack from outside, which could mean we're at war." She glanced out the window. "Wouldn't we know if we were at war?"

"Maybe not. If someone had hacked into our systems, they could do that from the other side of the world."

"But again, what would they gain?"

Keme simply shrugged. He had some ideas, but no real evidence to back up those suppositions. "Or it could be a natural disaster."

"Akule said GPS isn't working, but the cars are...so, not a solar flare."

"No, not that."

"What else is there?"

"What we don't know about space far exceeds what we think we do know."

Lucy dropped her head into her hands. "I just wanted to enjoy my summer vacation."

He stood, walked behind her, and rubbed her shoulders.

Finally, she straightened her posture and tilted her head back to look at him. "Thank you."

He kissed her lips, then began clearing the table.

"I guess I might as well work in the garden today. If the apocalypse is indeed here, we'll need fresh vegetables." She sighed. "That was supposed to be a joke, but...not funny."

"Stay positive, Professor Lopez. I expect you to be quoting poetry by noon."

"I'll need a second cup of instant coffee for that."

The lights suddenly came on. With a squeal, Lucy popped a pod into the coffee maker, which did its thing and produced the perfect cup of java.

"What are you going to do today?" She smiled at him over the brim of her favorite mug.

"Think I'll go and talk to our neighbors."

They had two neighbors, one living on each side of their place. John lived to the north. Franklin's place was to the south. The three trailers comprised the entire neighborhood, if that's what you wanted to call it. They said hello when passing and respected each other's privacy. They were neighborly enough to loan a power tool or help with a flat tire, but they didn't sit around in each other's back yard enjoying barbeques. Keme wasn't sure why. Maybe it was the fact that he didn't drink. It made some people nervous, and Franklin, in particular, enjoyed his beer.

He walked first to one trailer and then the other. Neither man was home. Franklin was divorced and lived alone except for a big mutt who spent most of his time in the back yard. Keme gave Teddy a pat on the head, made sure he had water, and headed over to John's. John was younger and lived with his wife, Betsy. Both worked from home, and if they'd explained what it was they did, Keme had forgotten.

"John went into town," Betsy explained. "He's pretty worried."

"You guys have enough food and stuff?"

"Sure. I guess." Betsy held her long blonde hair up off her neck. "It's so stinking hot. Why do these things happen in the dead of summer or the dead of winter?"

Keme shrugged. "Tell John I came by?"

"Sure."

"And, Betsy, holler if you need anything."

"Okay."

They were probably in their early 30s, but to Keme both Betsy and John seemed impossibly young which was a pretty funny thought since he was only forty-two. A vast amount of ground lay between his 30s and forty-two. It was ground he would not want to cover again.

Keme spent the rest of the day going through things in the shed, looking for anything that could be useful. He found a compound bow he'd messed around with and forgotten about, more camping supplies that he hadn't used since Paco was a teenager, and an old .22 hunting rifle. At the very back of the shed he found a trunk of things from his grandfather. He squatted in front of it, opened the latch, and was immediately carried into the past by the sight and smell of what lay there.

A book on how to make animal snares.

A hunting knife.

An old cane fishing pole, broken down into three pieces.

A turkey call.

An axe.

A coil of rope.

An old pair of Bushnell binoculars.

He remembered teasing his grandfather about keeping all of this stuff. An animal snare? Who needed an animal snare? But as he pulled the trunk out into the sun, removed and cleaned each item, he thought that perhaps his grandfather had been the wise one after all.

On Thursday the lights flickered one last time, then went out for good. Keme and Lucy were again sitting out on the front porch when John walked down their driveway.

"Hey. I came over to see you..." Keme rose to meet the man, shook his hand.

John was lanky and pale, and his brown hair fell into his eyes. "Yeah, Betsy told me. I wanted to let you know that we're leaving."

Keme exchanged a glance with Lucy. "Where are you headed? For how long?"

"Big Bend and then...depending what we find...across."

"Mexico?" Lucy stood, moved beside Keme. "Why, John? What's in Mexico?"

He didn't answer right away, and that was how Keme knew that he'd thought long and hard about this. He was trying to put all of that reasoning into as succinct a statement as possible. Finally he simply smiled and said, "Seems like a good place to be when society collapses."

"Wait...the power's out. That doesn't mean..." Lucy stopped, pulled in a deep breath, and muttered "men" with a shake of her head.

"Power's out. Internet's out. From what I've heard the grocery store shelves are empty. And no federal officials have shown up to take over the train crash scene. Put it all together, and I'd rather leave early than later."

"Betsy's okay with this?" Keme asked.

"Yeah. We're going to consider it a *Grand Adventure.*" He put figurative quote marks around the last two words. "If things improve, what have we lost? A couple weeks hiking in the Chisos Mountains."

"Okay. Well, good luck, man."

"You're staying?"

"Yeah. We are."

"Anything at my place you need, help yourself. The key is in that little mouse thing by the front door."

"Got it." Keme shook his head, not quite believing they'd arrived at this point this quickly. But then, he'd bought hundreds of dollars worth of food, medicine, and ammo, so who was he to judge another man's plan? "But if we borrow anything, I'll keep a list, and we'll settle up when you get back."

"Solid plan."

They shook again, John waved at Lucy, and then he was gone.

"Wow," Lucy said.

"Yup."

"I wonder what's going to happen next."

Which was exactly what Keme was thinking.

On Friday their other neighbor left. Franklin was going to try and connect with family in San Angelo. He loaded his big dog into the front passenger seat. Boxes of food, ammunition, and clothing filled the floorboards.

"Looks like you got it all," Keme said, standing beside the man's truck. It was a king cab and probably only got fifteen miles to a gallon. Keme noticed two gas cans in the truck's bed. "Did you fill those up?"

"I did, though I shouldn't need them just to get to San Angelo. The tank's full." Franklin had a love for fast food and had gained a good fifty pounds since Keme had known him. Now he stood there, hands on his hips, staring at the bed of his truck, trying to figure out what he might have forgotten.

"You going up through Fort Stockton?"

That jerked Franklin's attention back to the present moment. "No. I heard Fort Stockton is pretty chaotic."

"You heard that on your shortwave?"

"Yeah, when it was working. Now it isn't receiving anything, which I don't understand."

"Maybe there's just nothing to receive."

"You think they're all dead?"

"I think there aren't that many people with short-wave radios, and some of the ones who are...well they aren't going to broadcast. They're survivalists and they're worried you're going to triangulate their location, then show up in the middle of the night and steal their stuff."

Franklin reached into the truck, pulled out his map, and opened it on the hood. Teddy was in the front seat, staring at them, waiting patiently, ready to ride shotgun.

"Fort Stockton's no good, and I'm expecting that I-10 may ...well, it may not be safe." He found Alpine on the map, followed

I-90 east to Dryden and then Highway 349 north. "Thought I'd cross I-10 here, at Sheffield. Usually isn't any traffic there."

"I can see why you bought the extra gas."

"I bought the gas because there may not be any more." He reached into his pocket and pulled out a folded, letter-sized envelope. "I jotted down a map to my in-law's place on the back. Take it. If you ever go that direction, stop by."

"Look. I'm with you on this. Something has happened. Something more than just a train wreck. Lucy thinks it's another of my conspiracy theories, but..."

Franklin carefully refolded the map, then tossed it into the truck. "Train wrecks don't cause cell phones to go down, or crash the internet, or stop food deliveries."

"Exactly." Keme reached out and touched his shoulder. "You don't have to do this. You can ride it out, here, with us. With me and Lucy."

He was surprised when Franklin looked up at him and smiled, then pulled him into a bro hug. "I always knew you were one of the good ones."

One of the good ones?

"But I've got family in San Angelo." He hopped into the truck, pulling a handgun out of his pants pocket and set it on the passenger seat. "My ex. My kids. Even my sister is in San Angelo. That's where I need to be. And the extra gas? We'll use it to barter if we have to."

"Take care, man."

"Yeah, you too."

Franklin gave a small wave, then he and Teddy were gone.

Saturday morning Keme and Lucy woke to what felt like an earthquake.

This time when they walked out to the overlook, he took his binoculars. He and Lucy took turns looking through them, but saw nothing out of the ordinary.

Keme wanted to go after Akule, but Lucy disagreed.

"She came by yesterday, Keme. She's fine."

"Today isn't yesterday. Today's worse. We don't even know what that explosion or earthquake was."

"Our daughter has a good head on her shoulders. She'll come home if she needs to. We have to let her stand on her own, Keme. Even during this."

Late Sunday afternoon, Tanda arrived—riding a horse.

"Tanda." Lucy walked out on the porch and embraced her.

Keme's wife and sister were the same height, but Lucy was rounder, softer. Tanda didn't carry any extra pounds. Since she'd taken the job as police chief, her figure had grown even more wiry, and now with this...well, he was worried about what the weight of it all would do to her.

"It's good you came," Lucy said as they walked into the trailer. "We've been worried about you."

Tanda laughed. "Mom's worried about Keme. Sent me here to check on him."

"It's not me you need to check on." Keme stood between the kitchen and the living room.

He watched Tanda assess him—look for any suggestion that he might be backsliding. It didn't make him defensive. He realized he was lucky to have someone as dependable as Tanda keeping an eye on him. She was the best sponsor he could hope for.

Tanda returned his hug. They both had their mother's dark hair and brooding eyes—Indian eyes. Keme had inherited their father's height. All that Tanda had inherited from their pop was his Spanish temper.

"Who should I be checking on then?"

"Your government. Make no mistake that they are behind this."

Lucy wagged her hands back and forth in mock frustration. "You talk to him, and maybe he'll stop pestering me with his conspiracy theories."

"Pestering? When Alpine has been scattered away like so much dust, you'll be depending on me to bring you rabbit for dinner."

"Lucy's a better shot than you are, Keme."

"And now you gang up on me." But he smiled, grateful for the moment of banter.

Tanda followed him back into the kitchen, and the three sat down for a cup of coffee. He noticed her checking to see that he'd properly cracked the window near the camp stove. "You don't have to worry about us."

"So I see."

They spoke of food supplies, their parents, Abuela, and finally his neighbors.

"They're both gone."

"Any idea where they went?"

"John was headed south to Big Bend. Said it was the best place to be when society collapses."

"John always was an optimist."

"Franklin was going to try to connect with family in San Angelo."

Tanda studied her coffee, then downed the rest of it. "I hope they make it."

"As do we."

"Any word from Paco or Akule?"

"Paco called before the train crash, but we haven't heard from him since. Akule stopped by yesterday. She seemed okay."

"What about Sul Ross?"

Lucy shrugged. "You know I don't teach summer courses."

"But has the school sent out an email…"

They all smiled. It was so easy to slip back into the old way of thinking.

Lucy stood and gathered up the coffee cups. "I'm going to tend to my garden. We'll need the fresh vegetables more than ever. Tanda, you come stay with us if you need to."

"Thank you."

Keme knew that wasn't going to happen.

When the front screen door had slapped shut after Lucy, Keme stood. "There's something I want to show you."

He took her into his office and methodically went through the screenshots from the morning of the train crash, from the moment when everything had changed. He didn't know if it would make any more sense to her than it had to him, but he did know that the answer was somehow in those screenshots.

And whatever they needed to be prepared for?

That was there too.

Chapter 1

T HE FIRST INDICATION THAT the world had changed happened at 11:02 on a Tuesday morning in June. Tanda Lopez was sitting at her desk when the passenger train travelling from Marfa to Marathon collided with the freight train out of Fort Stockton. The explosion rattled the windows of the police station in their little town of Alpine. Birds startled from the trees. Car alarms blared throughout the town.

Tanda's heart beat a double tap.

"Makowski, Grant...you're with me."

"You got it, Chief."

They sped toward the site. It wasn't a head-on collision, but it was bad enough. The Amtrak train had sideswiped the end of the freight train. It looked as if the timing of one or the other train had been off by less than a minute. They spent the next nine hours directing emergency triage. A few times she tried to call the station, but inexplicably the radios were out.

That should have been her second clue. Why would the radio system be down? There was no way it was related to the train crash.

Yet, the chances of two separate events happening in their small rural town simultaneously were too unlikely to calculate.

"I'm headed back into town, if you can spare me."

Dixie Peters nodded as she directed two of her fire personnel toward a hot spot. "What do you think caused it?"

"I have no idea."

"Why is no one else here? We should have received help from Fort Davis and Fort Stockton."

"I don't have any ideas about that either."

"But it's strange, right?" Dixie swiped blonde hair out of her eyes.

"Yeah. It's strange."

It was more than strange. It was off.

The horror of sixty tons of passenger train smashing into three hundred tons of freight train had numbed Tanda's normally sharp instincts. She wasn't thinking about the radios. She was thinking about the wreckage, the debris, the bodies, and the cries for help. Those nine hours were among the longest in her life, or so she thought at the time.

She couldn't have known what lay ahead.

She wouldn't have wanted to know. A few more hours of ignorance, it turned out, might have been a good thing.

Tanda left Makowski and Grant to deal with the site clean-up and body bags. She headed back to headquarters as the sun dipped toward the horizon, casting shadows across the west Texas landscape. She drove toward the station, but her mind kept slipping back to the disaster behind her, to the people whose lives had so suddenly and tragically ended. Something else nagged at her and pulled her thoughts to the scene outside her police cruiser. Something else needed her attention, but she couldn't quite pinpoint what that something was.

Driving down Fifth Street, she had the distinct impression that she'd stepped into the past.

Alpine was a small town—only six thousand folks. Their traffic lights consisted of flashing reds at the two busiest intersections. She slowed as she encountered the first signal that wasn't working, and then the next. The entire system was down.

Few if any cars were on the road.

Stores were closed. That was par for the course at eight in the evening on a Tuesday. Small Texas towns still rolled up at five o'clock sharp.

So why were so many people out on foot? She'd expected the gawkers at the train wreck, and they'd had the usual group of those. This was different though. This had nothing to do with that. People were literally everywhere—sitting on park benches, standing outside of closed stores, even walking in the middle of the road.

Several times she had to tap her horn in order to alert a resident to move out of her lane. They barely acknowledged her as they trudged to the middle of the street—phones held high, attention glued to the devices in their hands.

There was a line at the town's single ATM, which didn't seem to be working. The windows on her cruiser were rolled down, and the temperature—even at sunset—hovered in the eighties. She could clearly hear the expletives hurled at the cash machine. Tempers were flaring and frustration was high.

Then she passed the Grocery Mart. Their only grocery store was run by Todd and Nona Jane. It had apparently closed early, a good two hours early. The only other time she could remember them closing before ten p.m. was on 9-11. That had been a Tuesday too. Tanda had been thirteen years old when the World Trade Center towers fell. It was when she'd first known that she wanted to be a police officer.

She could have stopped her cruiser, could have asked someone what was going on, but one glance at the expression on the faces of the folks she passed told her they didn't know what was happening either. On that Tuesday, no one could have known or even guessed.

Tanda didn't stop. She continued to headquarters instead. She had to park in the adjacent lot because theirs was full. She walked into a room packed with agitated residents huddled under the fluorescent lights. Some were shouting at each other, a few hollered at her, and the rest simply milled about.

Why?

Why were they here?

Conor Johnson was manning the front desk. He seemed to be the only officer in the building.

"My office. Now."

He jumped up and sprinted after her.

"I wasn't exactly sure what to do, but since there was no way to call you, I just held the line. That's what they taught us in training. Hold the line and—"

"Wait." She shut the door, dropped into her chair and snagged a drink out of the small refrigerator she kept near her desk. Popping the tab of the Coke, she took the first gulp before she realized it was lukewarm. Their receptionist, Edna, had left a note on her desk.

Keme stopped by.
Wanted you to know he would check
on your parents and your niece.

Why was her brother checking on their parents and his daughter?

She looked up, realized Conor was still waiting. "Continue."

"Comms are out."

"Which ones?"

"All of them. Land lines work, but I tried contacting the station in Marathon and the call wouldn't go through. Only local calls work, I guess. Cell phones aren't working either."

"All of our radios are out?"

"Yes."

She'd hoped only hers was out or that something around the wreckage had interrupted communications. She hadn't even considered that the entire system was down. She made a motion with her hand for him to continue and guzzled the rest of the drink. It tasted terrible, but she suddenly needed both the caffeine and the sugar. She wished for something stronger, then pushed that thought away. The bottle of Jim Bean in the bottom drawer of her filing cabinet was for celebrations—not catastrophes.

Not for days when she had to help zip bodies into bags. Something told her whiskey wouldn't help erase those images in her mind. Something else told her the worst was yet to come.

"Televisions are out, satellite radio, internet...it's all down. The electricity has gone out a few times, but it always comes back on."

That explained the warm soda. "Anything else?"

"The rest...I didn't leave my post, so I only know what folks are saying."

"Which is?"

"Everything's stopped working. I mean, like I said, electricity is working now—" He glanced up at the overhead lights and hesitated as if praying that they'd stay on.

"Conor?"

"Right. Uh...the ATM is out so we have a crowd over at the machine even though that's obviously useless. A good third of the people in our lobby are lost tourists."

"Lost?"

"GPS is out, and you know...they don't have a map. Probably couldn't read one even if they did."

"Why is the Grocery Mart closed?"

The single grocery store was a lifeline for their small community. The last thing they needed was panic buying. People in west Texas tended to over-prepare if they heard a storm was coming. Mention snow and ice, and the shelves in the bread aisle would empty in under an hour.

"Mrs. Crowder stopped by to check on us and according to her, Todd closed the mart because they couldn't take payments, plus apparently there was a run on what was stocked. A lot of panic buying."

Of course there was. Did people think a train wreck would keep the delivery trucks from arriving? What else was happening here?

"Do we have anyone on it?"

"Rodriguez headed over to the store when we heard there'd been shots fired."

Tanda wanted to drop her head into her hands, but she didn't. She simply stared at Conor. He was her newest recruit, a lanky five foot, ten inches, and definitely still damp behind the ears. He'd held his position though—*held the line*. Maybe he was going to make it as an officer after all.

Conor seemed to have run out of things to say.

Tanda reached for the mouse on her computer, jiggled it once, and clicked on the internet browser, but Conor shook his head.

"Internet's out. Remember?"

"Right." She leaned back in her chair, studied him, then turned her attention to the group of people still gathered past the glass wall of her office. "Has the mayor issued a statement?"

"Not that I've heard, but she sent Ben Cason over with this."

Tanda tried not to grimace as she reached for the slip of paper. If there was one person she didn't play well with, it was their newly elected mayor, Melinda Stone. Ben Cason was a close second.

My office. Eight o'clock. Don't be late.

"Tomorrow?"

"Tonight."

"I'm already late."

"Cason was pretty adamant about your being there, though I told him I had no way to make you aware unless I left my post—which I wasn't about to do."

Tanda nodded, chunked her soda can into the recycle bin, and stood. "Can you stay?"

"Of course."

"Need a break?"

"Maybe three minutes to use the..." He nodded toward the restroom, apparently too embarrassed to say the word *urinal*.

She gestured that he was excused. Johnson was at the door before he asked the question she'd expected from the moment she'd walked in. "How many casualties?"

"Eight dead, another two dozen injured."

Conor's eyes widened. "Where did you take them?"

"Critical cases went to our local medical center, but most of our docs are out of town for that conference in Dallas. Doc Fielder is doing the best he can. Anyone whose injuries allowed for transport were sent to Fort Stockton."

"Their EMS showed up?"

"No. They didn't."

Which was another thing that should have raised alert bells in her mind. As Dixie had pointed out, they should have had help by now. Why hadn't any neighboring EMS units shown up? Fort

Stockton was 50 percent bigger, largely owing to its being situated on Interstate 10. They had an EMS three times the size of Alpine's, and they had a better staffed medical center.

Fort Stockton should have picked up the chatter over the radios—only the radios were out. It was probably too far away for them to have heard the actual crash, but surely someone would have told someone else. It was the way things worked in their remote section of west Texas.

But they hadn't shown up. Alpine was left to handle the disaster on their own. They had only three ambulances, which had always been enough. Dr. Fielder had sent two to Fort Stockton, leaving one to ferry the injured to their own understaffed medical center. When the two that went to Stockton didn't return, they'd resorted to using people's vans and trucks.

Why hadn't the EMS people returned?

Sweat broke out on her forehead, and it wasn't from the heat. A wave of fear swept over her. She'd been with the department for ten years and had been promoted to chief three years ago.

She knew how to swallow past that fear.

Knew what was expected of her.

She needed to figure out what was happening. Then they could formulate a plan to deal with it.

Conor headed toward the men's room, and Tanda walked back out to the reception desk. At only five foot, four inches, she couldn't even see over the front row of people. But Tanda understood that presence was about more than height. She found the stepping stool that their receptionist used for filing in the top drawers, moved it in front of Conor's station, and stepped onto it. She thought she might have to use her whistle, but raising her hand was enough. The crowd quieted, all eyes pinned on her.

"If you've come here for answers, I don't have them. Obviously, there's been an event of some sort..."

"I heard it was aliens." Dylan Spencer was sitting on her worktable, his jean-clad butt right next to her coffee pot, NRA cap pulled low and a gun on his hip.

She didn't call him on the gun because she knew that he had a permit to carry.

She didn't tell him to get the hell out of her station because he was the local football hero, only four years out of high school, and that sort of thing held a lot of weight.

"Let me know if you come across one, Dylan. I'll come out myself and question him or her. Or it."

That earned her a few grunts of approval and one or two laughs.

The tension which threatened to permeate the room temporarily receded, then rushed back in.

"Why's everything not working? Is it because of the train wreck?" Moses Carter had lived in Alpine longer than anyone she knew. The man had to be nearing the century mark.

"Mr. Carter, I don't see how those two things could be related, but I don't have any other explanation either. We're going to figure this out. When we do, I'll let you know. Until then, I need everyone to go home."

"But we can't even call 9-1-1 if we need help." This from one of the elderly women who lived over in the sixty-five-and-up apartments.

"Officer Johnson isn't going anywhere. He's going to stay right here." Fortunately, at that moment Conor appeared at his desk.

Tanda turned around in time to see him give everyone a small wave, then the group in front of her waved back.

"If you have an emergency, you send someone here and Conor will take care of you."

She didn't add that Conor had no way to call for an officer, let alone dispatch one.

These people looked frightened enough.

Those sorts of details could wait until daylight, when, with a little bit of luck, everything would be working again.

"How are we supposed to get home?" This from a skinny twenty-year-old wearing a University of Texas tee, who repeatedly combed his fingers through his scraggly goatee. No doubt he'd arrived in the sports car she'd seen parked in her spot. "Our GPS doesn't work," he added.

"There are only two roads out of Alpine, sir. Sixty-seven goes east and west; 118 goes north and south. Where are you headed?"

"Austin."

That brought a few snickers from the locals.

Logan Wright raised his hand. He was standing at the back of the crowd, and Tanda wondered why he was there. Logan had grown up in Alpine, gone off to Texas A&M University to earn his veterinary degree, and come back home to open up their only animal clinic. He'd been practicing twenty years, and she'd never once seen him even slightly stumped. Not when someone had brought him a baby camel that needed vaccinating. Not even the time they'd found a seven-foot alligator living in a resident's garage.

"I can help anyone who needs directions."

Tanda nodded her thanks. "Mr. Wright will meet you out in front of the building."

"But we can't even purchase gas," a middle-aged mom said.

"Why is that, ma'am?"

"The station attendant said they couldn't take our credit cards...something about the system being down."

"Are they taking cash?"

"Well, yes, but..."

Tanda interrupted her before she could list her problems one by one. "Officer Johnson will help you if you need cash in order to purchase fuel. This isn't a hand-out, people. You'll be expected to repay the amount you receive within thirty days. If you need assistance, leave your contact information with him. He can front you enough to get you to the next town. Hopefully by then, the credit card system will be up and running again."

Turning to Conor, she lowered her voice and said, "Use the petty cash. If that runs out, I keep some extra in the third drawer of my desk."

Everyone began talking and moving. Tanda headed toward the rear entrance, toward her cruiser. Then she remembered she'd parked it across the street. She turned around to exit through the front door, and Logan stepped out with her after assuring his group of lost motorists that he'd be right back.

"Walk you to your car?"

"Sure, Logan. Why not?"

"Status of the train wreck?"

She told him, unsure why he needed to know that now but trusting he wouldn't ask unless he did.

He hesitated, then muttered, "Something's not right here."

"Understatement of the year."

She'd reached her car, opened the door, and sank into the seat. Logan stopped her from closing the door and crouched down beside her so they were eye to eye.

She wanted to reach out and smooth the skin above his right eye, the place where the scar was. He'd told her the story once. He was in veterinary school. Was thinking about his professor, who was watching him assess an old gelding. He'd approached from behind, frightened the animal, and earned a solid kick. Fortunately, the kick had missed his eye.

"Something's not right."

"EMP?" She'd seen enough apocalyptic TV to know the usual culprits—nuclear blast, EMP, meteor. The first and last seemed unlikely since they were sitting there talking, but the middle one was a possibility.

"I don't think so." He reached out, tapped her steering wheel. "This probably wouldn't work if we'd been hit by an EMP."

"Anything you know that I don't?"

"A lot." Now he smiled and stood. "But not about this."

"Well, when you do, you know where to find me."

She started her cruiser, suddenly grateful that it worked, and drove the three blocks to city hall, to her meeting with the mayor, and hopefully toward some answers.

Chapter 2

TANDA HAD NO DELUSIONS about the meeting she'd been ordered to attend. She'd never seen eye-to-eye with the mayor. She doubted that would change because of their current emergency.

Melinda Stone somehow managed to appear as if everything was situation normal. Her attire included designer red heels and a black power suit with red piping. The blonde streaks in her hair had been carefully styled, and she was even wearing her customary diamond necklace and hoop earrings. Stone was the kind of fifty-year-old woman who was determined to look thirty. How she'd become mayor was something Tanda still puzzled over late at night. It was also a source of contention between Alpine's artist community, who were mostly out-of-state people, and the ranching community who had been born and raised in the surrounding area.

"Nice of you to join us, Chief."

Stone sat at the head of the conference table. There was never any doubt as to who was running a meeting if Melinda Stone was in attendance.

Tanda stood just inside the doorway, doing a quick survey of the room.

Ben Cason sat to the mayor's immediate right. Ben had once been on the correct side of things, but he'd fallen under the mayor's spell the year before.

Ron Mullins from Public Works.

Fire Chief Dixie Peters—how had Dixie beat her here? Stone must have sent someone to drag her away from the crash site.

Emmanuel Garcia with County Health.

Ben had apparently been scribbling meeting notes on the large white board. Tanda flash backed to their third-grade teacher trying to teach Ben to write in a straight and proper manner. She'd keep him at the board, practicing, through recess and even lunch. Twenty-five years later, and his penmanship hadn't improved. Each line item on the whiteboard tilted precariously to the right, as if the words were ready and willing to dive onto the carpet.

No interruptions in water, minor electric outages.

Crews on standby.

No fires or major accidents, other than train collision.

No regional or state-wide emergency health notices.

Stone steepled her fingers together and peered down the long table at Tanda. "Care to update us on your department, Chief Lopez?"

After a twelve-hour shift, Tanda was tired and dirty, and she was still seeing images of the mangled bodies she'd helped bag and tag. She wanted to be home taking a hot bath, washing off the grit and blood. She did not want to be here, playing Stone's games. The items on the board were ludicrous.

"Officers Grant and Makowski are still at the train site, helping with casualties. Rodriquez is at the Grocery Mart trying to keep the good folks of Alpine from rioting. Johnson's at the station watching over a crowd of people who are scared and asking questions I can't answer. A good number of tourists are lost because their GPS won't work."

"Well." The mayor sniffed. "It sounds for once as if your department has things under control."

"Under control? Nothing is under control."

"There's no need to be dramatic, Chief."

Tanda knew she should sit down and shut up. She should keep her cool. But she kept seeing the look of concern and befuddlement on Logan's face. She kept hearing him say, "Something's not right here."

The mayor had moved on, saying that she expected everyone to be at their posts the next day, on time, business as normal. It was important to maintain a calm and coordinated front to the people.

Tanda only half heard. She walked to the front of the room and picked up the marker that Ben had been using. Stone stopped talking and threw her a questioning look.

Holding up the marker, Tanda asked, "Do you mind?" She practically dared the woman to try and stop her.

Stone dismissively waved a hand at the board.

Pulling in a deep breath, Tanda drew a question mark next to the first item.

No interruptions in water, minor electric outages.

"Why are the traffic lights out, Ron?"

He cleared his throat, his gaze darting from Stone to Tanda. "We believe it's a computer malfunction, but we're...uh... unable to talk to web support at this time."

"Because the phones are out?"

"Right."

"And the internet is out."

"Right." Ron squirmed in his seat. "Of course, the internet and phones aren't technically in my department."

Tanda didn't bother responding to that.

"Do we know what caused the train crash?"

"There will be a proper investigation, but it could be months before we have definitive answers."

"I was at the train site all day. There was no one from the Federal Railroad Administration there."

"That would be...unusual." Ron looked toward the mayor as he said this.

Tanda understood that Ron was six months away from retirement. He hadn't voted for Stone. He'd shared that piece of information with Tanda that one night at the local pub. His plan was to lie low, not antagonize the mayor, and retire the first day he was eligible to do so.

Stone was looking at Tanda as if she wanted to snatch away the marker and claw her eyes out with those ruby-red nails. Tanda shrugged and tapped the next item on the white board.

"Dixie, did the two ambulances we sent out make it back?"

Dixie shook her head.

"Any word from them?"

"No, but that doesn't mean anything. Phones are down. Maybe they just got tied up doing paperwork."

"Eight dead and over two dozen injured. I think they would have known to save the paperwork until end of shift."

"If the receiving facility let them, sure, but..."

"Why didn't any of the neighboring municipalities respond?"

Dixie shrugged. She'd been in the job two years and was the first female fire chief in Alpine, probably in west Texas. She'd done a bang-up job, but she was in over her head.

They all were.

Ben tapped his pen against his ever-present pad of paper, as if to hurry her along.

Emmanuel looked braced for her question, as if he could defend not having received any health warnings. Instead, Tanda asked, "Do we still have the emergency management supplies? Food, water, meds..."

"Sure, but..."

"But what?"

"Some of it expired and had to be tossed. I put in a request to replenish supplies, but I haven't heard anything on that yet. Guess it got stuck in the paperwork pipeline somewhere."

Tanda stared down at the new carpet in the redecorated conference room. How much money had been spent on that? Where was the mayor even finding funds for redecorating?

Something's not right here.

She stared at the board, though her words were directed to Emmanuel. "Maybe you should get someone to check into that first thing tomorrow."

Stone stood and snatched the marker from Tanda's hand. "Thank you, Chief Lopez. I'm sure everyone here appreciates your clarifying those points, but as I was saying, it's important that we continue a business-as-usual demeanor..."

"You cannot be serious."

"I am serious, and you are out of order." Stone's voice had gone low, cold, hard.

"Logan Wright thinks there's something happening, something bigger than..."

"I don't think we need to resort to asking advice on how to run a city from a country vet." Stone walked back to the conference table, smirking, practically laughing.

Could the woman be even half as arrogant as she appeared?

"And I don't think you have any idea what you're doing."

"Stop." Stone's hand came down hard on the table, causing the water in the glass in front of her to jump. "I will not tolerate your insubordination today of all days."

"Huh. Okay. When you decide you're ready to do some real city planning, send Ben over with another note. Until then, I have work to do."

And with those words, which would probably eventually result in her termination, she walked out of the room and to her cruiser. She drove through the Sonic and picked up two coffees and two burgers. As she paid—with cash—the car hop informed her that the latest rumor was that Alpine had been picked for a government experiment. A bubble had been placed over the town to see how they would fare if no one could get in or out, which sounded like the plot line of a horror book she'd read.

Tanda figured she'd passed exhaustion because as she drove back toward the train wreckage she could picture Stone on the phone with a covert agency, one with an alphabet soup name, offering Alpine to the highest bidder.

She dropped the burgers and coffee off with Makowski and Grant, then set off to find Jorge. Officer Rodriguez was a veteran officer with more years' experience than herself. She'd worried there might be some animosity when she was offered the position of chief, but Rodriguez had assured her that he wasn't interested. He loved his job, but he had a wife and five children. He didn't want the extra hours or the extra responsibility—and they both knew it wasn't worth the measly extra pay.

She needed to find him and assess what was happening at the Grocery Mart. The good people of Alpine had most likely gone home for the night, but come morning, they needed to see that their local grocer was open. One way or another, she was going to make that happen. If she couldn't, if residents couldn't buy milk or bread and they couldn't use their cell phones, she would very likely have a riot to deal with.

Chapter 3

T ANDA MANAGED TO EXACT a promise from Todd and Nona Jane that they would open the next day and stay open as long as there was anything left to sell. She helped them come up with guidelines, which she had Conor write up on three pieces of poster board.

Limit of 10 people in the store at a time.

CASH only.

5 items per person.

No duplicate items.

They taped one poster to the entrance and the other two down the outer east wall where there was space for a line to queue up. Tanda promised to provide security.

She held a meeting with her department at two in the morning. The muscle above her left eye had begun to twitch, something that hadn't happened since she'd taken finals in college. She pressed a finger above her eye, trying to still the muscle as Makowski and Grant walked into the room—finally back from the train wreck.

Grant sank into a chair and provided the update. "There's still debris all over the place, Chief. No one came to help move it, and well...it's a train. It's not like we could lift it and put it back on the track. The bodies, we took to the morgue."

They looked exhausted and more than a little shell-shocked.

Conor looked as if he might fall asleep in his chair. They'd finally managed to clear the waiting area of residents and tourists.

Theirs was a small department in a small town. Tanda had four officers under her supervision—Grant, Johnson, Makowski and Rodriguez. Their usual schedule was for three officers to be on during the day, one at night, and one scheduled off. She worked the same hours as any other officer, plus tended to any administrative tasks.

This was different, though. This was an all-hands-on-deck situation. Only, some of the hands looked battle fatigued and exhausted.

Tanda had promised Todd and Nona Jean a police presence for the fifteen hours they would attempt to remain open—from seven in the morning until ten at night. She had a total of five officers if she included herself, which she did. Jorge Rodriguez offered to take the first four hours at the store. Every other officer would take a three-hour shift.

"Hopefully Edna will be in to man the phones—"

"Which still aren't working," Conor pointed out.

"Right. But it will help to have her here at her regular time to take over the front desk. In fact, I'll call..." Tanda mentally slapped her forehead.

Conor had the presence of mind to not correct her again.

"I'll stop by her place on my way home," Tanda said. "Ask her to come in a couple hours early. Conor, I want you off for at least six hours."

They should be able to resort to their regular schedule once everyone had managed a few hours of sleep. Alpine was a small town with an even smaller police department, but she had a good group of officers. If they could keep the population calm, sidestep Stone, institute temporary measures—they could push through until things returned to normal.

But how long would that take?

Two days?

Three?

The following days passed in something of a blur. On Wednesday the electricity continued to flicker, and it was completely off by Thursday morning. Stone sent two city workers to Marfa, two more to Fort Davis, and a final two to Marathon. None of them returned. There was still no word from the ambulances that had left on Tuesday. Strangely, the phones that were landlines came back on, but only local calls could go in or out.

The water shut off Thursday afternoon, and the Grocery Mart closed on the same day—this time because there was nothing left to sell. Later that evening Dr. Fielder died of a heart attack. To Tanda it felt as if the punches were coming so hard and fast that she barely had time to recover from them, let alone absorb them or respond in a measured way.

She spoke with Logan two more times. He didn't have any answers, though their questions were multiplying.

No one from FRA showed up to investigate the train crash. The crumpled cars remained scattered across the tracks, a reminder of the day the world changed.

On Friday morning, Tanda walked into the Alpine Police Department an hour before her shift began.

"Morning, Chief."

"Johnson."

Conor seemed the least phased by all that had happened. It was almost as if he had expected it. Was that what came from a generation raised on apocalyptic video games and disaster movies?

"What did I miss?"

She picked up the coffee carafe and felt the bottom of the glass. Cold.

"Power's still out."

"Still trying to make those calls?"

"Yup. Nothing's gone through. Occasionally I get a ringing that no one answers. Most of the time there's simply a click. I'm rotating through adjacent municipalities, state offices, and federal agencies."

Left unsaid was the question that was swiftly rising to the top of all others. Was there anyone out there? If so, why couldn't they reach them? Why had no one come to check on Alpine? Why was no one looking for those missing trains and missing people?

Their small town sat on a high plateau, at an elevation of 4500 feet, and surrounded by the Chihuahuan Desert. Their location was the crossroads of three scenic highways—67, 90, and 118. Fort Davis lay to the north, Marfa to the west, and Marathon to the east. All of them were smaller than Alpine. Big Bend National Park sat eighty miles to the south, on the border of Texas and Mexico, surrounded by 1100 square miles of desert.

They were isolated and in the dark.

"Any in-coming calls?"

"Only Mr. Grant." Simon Grant was one of the few residents of Alpine with a land line.

"And?"

"Heard something in the alley behind his house. Rodriguez went to check it out, then ride the circuit. He's due back in the next few minutes."

They'd switched to horses the day before. Each cruiser had a nearly full tank of gas, but Tanda had the distinct impression that they might need them for more important things than routine welfare checks. When would a fuel truck come through? What had actually happened? The lack of information was more than concerning. She'd give her left arm for five minutes on the internet.

No one was bartering Wi-Fi for body parts though, so she thanked Conor and walked into her office. She tried the light switch and was again surprised when nothing happened. Some habits stuck like gum to your shoe.

She'd been at her desk less than twenty minutes when Melinda Stone sailed through the open door and perched on the chair across from her. Somehow their mayor still managed to dress as if she were expected at a corporate board meeting. Did she have a generator that allowed her to steam clean her skirts and iron her blouse? Stone's only concession to the *situation* they were in...*situation* being as far as she was willing to go in accepting their current circumstances...was a color-coordinated, designer scarf tied around her hair.

"Mayor."

"Tanda, what are you doing about our medical emergency?"

"What would you like me to do about it?"

"Replace Fielder, obviously."

"The man's been dead less than twenty-four hours."

"Well unless you expect him to rise again, I don't see how the amount of time that has lapsed matters."

"And I don't see how it's my job to find a replacement."

"Fine. I'll put Cason on it." Stone popped out of her chair as if she had a dozen meetings to attend.

Tanda held up a hand. "Tell me what you want me to do." The only thing worse than doing Stone's bidding was knowing Cason was handling it. He wasn't corrupt as much as he was clueless. Tanda was learning that one could be as bad as the other.

Stone pulled a file folder from her Gucci shoulder bag and pushed it across Tanda's desk. "Get me this guy."

"Get him?"

"Dr. Miles Turner. He lives up Old Ranch Road."

Tanda leafed through the contents of the file—only a few sheets, but it held Dr. Turner's entire life.

"Where did you get this?"

"From my files."

"Why do you have it?"

Stone rolled her eyes, something that looked ridiculous on a woman of her age. "Does that really matter?"

"It does."

"We keep an eye on newcomers."

"He's been here a year. Well before you were in office."

"But not before I began my campaign. And stop looking at me that way. It's perfectly legal. Any person can run a background check on any other person. Besides, it's not as if court is in session. Court may never be in session again." She said it as if the idea didn't send a chill down her back, as if the lack of courts and legal process didn't concern her one bit. "He's hiding up there, and we need him down here. Promise him whatever you have to in order to convince him."

"What if he doesn't want to be convinced?"

"We both know how persuasive you can be, Tanda. If you have to, cast an Indian spell on him."

Tanda was too tired to be properly offended by the dig to her heritage. She didn't favor the mayor with a response.

"Just get him down here, before people realize that we're in the middle of a real crisis without a doctor."

Stone sailed out of the office much as she'd sailed in, leaving nothing behind except the faint scent of her perfume, which no doubt cost more than Tanda's entire gun belt.

"Johnson."

Conor appeared in her doorway with the enthusiasm of a Labrador puppy. "Whatcha need, Chief?"

"When Makowski gets back, tell him I want to see him."

"Sure thing."

She spent the next twenty minutes carefully reading the file Stone had dropped on her desk.

Miles Turner, age forty-one, graduated from Johns Hopkins with a medical degree and took a position at MD Anderson in Houston. The attached photo showed a Caucasian male with a strong profile and a touch of gray hair at the temples. Five foot, ten inches, one hundred and seventy-five pounds. Solid but not overly so. Happy. In the picture he looked happy. How many years ago had the photo been taken?

The next sheet explained that his wife and daughter had been killed three years earlier in a random shooting. Though the police had arrived on the scene as it was happening and captured the shooter, it took another two years for the perp's trial to proceed. He'd killed eight and injured three more.

Killed eight.

Tanda tapped her pen against the case summary.

The jury deliberated less than 90 minutes. Carl Bolin was currently incarcerated at the maximum-security prison in Huntsville, awaiting the day of his execution.

Dr. Turner had moved to the Alpine area eleven months ago and purchased a place on Old Ranch Road. There wasn't much out that way. Actually, there wasn't anything except scrub brush. What was he living in?

Obviously, he'd checked out of modern living.

Tanda didn't blame him, but now it was her job to bring him into the fold. She didn't want to do it. She'd rather leave him up there, nursing his wounds. But Stone was right—they needed a doctor.

Twenty minutes later she was in the saddle, riding Roxy. Stan Makowski sat easily atop a mare named Sofia. The day was warm, the sun already blazing. The horses were mostly used in parades and at stock shows. Tanda had the distinct feeling that the days of parades and stock shows were behind them.

If Roxy and Sofia were perturbed about the change in their routine, they didn't show it.

Stan Makowski was two years younger than Tanda, half a foot taller, and fifty pounds heavier. Like her, he'd never lived anywhere except Alpine. They both knew the backroads as well as the highways. More importantly, Stan was solid—physically and otherwise. She never had any doubt that he had her back.

In any situation, he was too willing to go to bat for her.

He would risk his life to save hers. There was no doubt about that. But Tanda didn't need saving. What she needed was an officer who could follow her lead and react quickly when the situation called for it. Stan could and would do both. On more than one occasion she'd promised his wife, Zoey, that she'd bring Stan back in one piece. They were expecting their fourth child.

"You really think you can bring him down?"

"I don't know," she admitted.

"I saw this guy once. At least I think it was him. He'd come to town to pick up chicken feed. Must have been last fall, when Zoey went on her natural kick and bought six hens. I guess she has the last laugh now."

"Stone says to promise Dr. Turner whatever it takes."

"What does that mean?"

"I honestly don't know."

"She have a storehouse of stuff we don't know about?"

"It wouldn't surprise me if she did."

The trip to Old Ranch Road would have taken seven minutes in the cruiser. Riding horseback, it took a good half hour. Tanda didn't mind. As they ascended the old caliche road, she stopped her mount, turned it, and looked back. In the distance, sunlight bounced off the train wreckage.

Stan pulled off his hat, wiped at the sweat trickling down his face, then resettled the hat. "Think we'll ever know what happened?"

"Yes. Someday I think we'll know."

"But not today."

"Nope."

Fifteen minutes later they took a narrow lane to the east. She'd never been down that particular lane. She certainly didn't realize there was an old log cabin or anyone living there. Then they rounded a bend where a man was standing on the front porch.

Miles Turner looked as if he was waiting for them.

Chapter 4

"S HE'S RIDDEN UP TO talk to the doctor."

"You're sure."

"Saw her leave myself. Took Stan Makowski with her."

Melinda Stone picked up her Montblanc pen and sat back in her chair. She studied the pen, turning it round and round. "I don't know exactly what we're facing, but my concern is that Chief Lopez won't be up to handling whatever lies ahead."

"She seems to be doing all right."

"*Seems to be* isn't quite as strong an endorsement as I'd like. We could be in a precarious position here, and now...now might be the moment to cement our place on top of the dog pile." She waved a hand, dismissing the person standing in front of her. "Keep your eyes and ears open. Report back to me tomorrow, or sooner if there's something I should know."

When she was alone in her office, Melinda stared out the second-story window. She hadn't wanted to come to this town. She certainly hadn't wanted to be mayor of it. Her husband, whom she'd divorced six months after arriving, had thought it was God's green acres. Looking out across Alpine now, she didn't see much green.

Gerald hadn't been surprised by the divorce. He'd packed up and moved without a fuss, claiming north and west was where all the action was.

He'd been mistaken about that.

There was plenty of action in this southwestern corner of Texas. People were literally flocking to the state in light of rising taxes and exorbitant land prices on the east and west coast. There was now a 27,000-acre resort in Lajitas, which included a PGA Championship golf course. That combined with a growing art community throughout the area, meant the entire southwest tip of Texas was primed for explosive growth.

Alpine was teetering on the tip of an economic boom.

Melinda found that the small town of Alpine had grown on her. She thought of it as her private little kingdom. People were surprisingly simple to manipulate, and they needed her. Left to their own devices, they'd scatter and starve like a litter of kittens whose mother had been run over on the side of the road.

That's where the analogy ended though, because she wasn't their mother and she didn't plan on being run over. She wasn't going anywhere.

This town needed her.

As for this present catastrophe, she would be surprised if it lasted another forty-eight hours. When the news crews rolled into town wanting the full and exclusive story, Melinda Stone would be there to greet them.

Chapter 5

MILES TURNER HADN'T HAD a single visitor since he'd moved into the old hunting cabin, which was fine with him. The cabin's isolated location was the reason he'd purchased it. He didn't want visitors. He didn't want to be reminded that for some, life continued to progress normally.

He also hadn't wanted a dog, but Zeus had adopted him. The mutt was definitely a Heinz 57, with a strong dose of Labrador. He'd alerted Miles to their visitors a good five minutes before they appeared in his clearing.

"Miles Turner? Dr. Miles Turner?" The woman looked to be in her thirties and was either Hispanic, Indian, or both. Her black hair was tied back and she wore an Alpine Police Department uniform, as did the rather large man at her side.

"I am." His voice sounded strange to his ears. How many days did he go without speaking? Unless he said something to Zeus, there was no need for words.

"I'm the Alpine Chief of Police, Tanda Lopez. This is Officer Stan Makowski."

Stan raised a hand in greeting, which Miles did not return.

"As police officers, I'm sure you both saw and understood the *No Trespassing* sign at the end of my lane."

"We need to speak with you, Dr. Turner."

"Why?"

"That's rather complicated. May we come in?"

He didn't want to invite them into his cabin, and he certainly wasn't going to offer them iced tea. He did, however, realize that the determined expression on the pretty face of Chief Lopez meant it would be quicker to hear her out than to argue, so he nodded.

They dismounted and tied their horses to a nearby cedar tree.

Miles didn't care why they were there, though he did wonder why they'd ridden horses instead of driving a cruiser. They followed him into the single-room cabin. The five-hundred-foot structure had been built a hundred years ago of native stone. It kept the heat out in the summer and the warmth in during the winter. This morning the temperature inside was a good ten degrees cooler than outside.

He only had the single chair, which he motioned her toward. Makowski stood at the door, arms crossed, eyes alert. Miles leaned against the kitchen counter, but he didn't speak.

He waited.

He'd become very good at waiting.

As the police chief studied him, he noticed the dark circles under her eyes. Insomniac? Alcoholic? People thought alcoholics slept a lot, and some did. Some passed out for long periods of time. Others found that after the initial buzz from their drink of choice, they were agitated and unable to sleep. Tanda Lopez was not agitated. She didn't jiggle a leg or fiddle with her hands.

She seemed uncertain as to how to begin the conversation.

"I have no idea what your *complicated* situation is, but I can assure you that I'll be no help."

"I hope that isn't true." She met his gaze, didn't blink, didn't look away. "Let's put that aside for now. Are you aware of the events of the last few days?"

He shrugged. A coyote had taken one of his chickens. His green bean plants were beginning to blossom, and he'd had to mend the fence on the back side of his property. He doubted she was referring to any of those things.

"Are you completely off the grid here?"

"I have a generator. Come to town once a month for diesel."

"Where do you get your water?"

"Natural spring in the back." He kept his answers short and to the point. He didn't see how any of this was her business, or what it could possibly have to do with her complicated situation.

"On Tuesday an Amtrak passenger train collided with a BNSF freight train. You didn't hear it?"

"I heard something. Didn't know it was a train."

"Eight were killed."

The number poked at him like a hot iron. He didn't answer her, didn't respond in any way.

"Another two dozen were injured."

"Is that what this is about?"

"You are a doctor."

How did she know that?

It didn't matter.

"I'm sure you have physicians in town who can handle the situation, or you could medivac them to San Angelo or Midland." Even as he spoke, he knew that could not be why she was here. Three days ago? The injured would be stabilized or dead by now.

"Authorities never came to investigate the crash. No one has arrived to pick up the bodies which we are now burying because there's no power to keep them refrigerated in the morgue. Communication, power, and water are out."

"From a train wreck?"

"We sent ambulances to Fort Stockton. They never returned. We also sent out three separate groups of city workers—in three different directions. They haven't been heard from either."

"I don't understand what you're telling me."

"Yeah. It's a little hard to grasp."

"Still haven't grasped it myself." Makowski adjusted his gun belt, no doubt relieving the pressure on his sciatica.

"We're doing the best we can, Dr. Turner, in a very unusual situation. Yesterday our only physician died."

"You only had one physician?"

"We had more, of course. All but Dr. Fielder were out of town at a conference." Tanda took in a single deep breath, and he understood that the circles under her eyes were from this weight she was carrying—the weight of Alpine.

"I can't help you."

"You're a physician. You graduated from Johns Hopkins and worked at MD Anderson."

"How do you know that?"

"Mayor Stone has asked me to come up and appeal to you."

"I don't practice medicine anymore."

"She's authorized me to promise you whatever compensation you need—"

"I don't want your money."

Chief Lopez didn't answer that. She waited.

Makowski finally said, "You'll need feed for your chickens and dog food. The stores shelves are empty, but Mayor Stone has said she'll provide whatever you need. All we're asking is that you come to town and help."

"I can't do that."

Lopez and Makowski stared at him. Miles didn't expect them to understand. How could they? But neither was he swayed by their story. Perhaps they were being overly dramatic. The situation couldn't be as bad as they described. Life didn't change that drastically in three days. But even as that thought passed through his mind, he realized that his had. One summer morning three years ago his life had changed irrevocably.

"I'd like you to leave."

Lopez exchanged a glance with Makowski and nodded once. He stepped outside, probably to fetch their horses. Miles walked out onto the porch, and Lopez had no choice but to follow.

"We wouldn't ask if we weren't desperate."

He didn't answer.

He didn't acknowledge what she'd said in any way.

"Makowski, he has three kids and his wife Zoey is due with their fourth next month. My *abuela* who is nearing ninety. She needs insulin every day, and I'm not sure what we're supposed to do when what we have runs out. We have six thousand souls in Alpine, and we need a doctor."

Miles ran his hand through his hair which now reached his collar. "It can't be as bad as you're describing."

"It is."

"What are they saying on the news?"

"There is no news, Dr. Turner. No internet. No information. We're flying blind here, and we're doing the best we can." She studied him a moment, then looked out over his property. "We need a physician. The only one we could find is you. I trust you'll at least think about it."

He shook his head once, hoped it portrayed with absolute certainty that he was not the man for the job. He wasn't the man for any job. Some days he couldn't even force himself to get out of bed. That happened less frequently than it had, but it still happened. The last thing he was capable of being was a doctor.

"Just think about it," she reiterated, and then she walked down his porch steps, mounted her horse, and she was gone.

Six thousand *souls*.

An interesting choice of words. That would be the Native American in her speaking—her root family's dialect. Did she believe in souls? Did she believe there was something beyond this? He stared out over the scrub brush until he saw the two horses carrying two riders come out of the turn and begin their descent down Old Ranch Road. He called to Zeus, retrieved a fishing pole from the shed, and walked to the pond at the back of his property.

A man still had to eat, even if the world had gone off the tracks. Not that he believed Chief Lopez. Something had happened, no doubt. And the part about needing a doctor—that rang true. But the rest? No internet or phones? He glanced up at the clear blue Texas sky. Perhaps there was some sort of satellite malfunction, but the government would clear it up.

No one needed his help.

He'd bet all the fish in his pond on that.

Chapter 6

TANDA WORKED THROUGH THE weekend. On Saturday there was a rumbling that she first thought was an earthquake. It lasted less than a minute. She was at the police department when another rumble caused the items on her bookshelf to fall over. Johnson stood in the doorway to her office, eyes wide and locked on the ceiling, as if he could focus hard enough to see what was happening.

It ended and they both let out a breath of relief.

"Any idea what that was, Chief?"

"None."

It was the not-knowing that set her teeth on edge. She told herself she could handle anything if she only knew what it was, but that might have been more wishful thinking than actual fact.

She took time off Sunday afternoon to visit her family. While riding Roxy to her parents, another rumbling occurred. This time she was able to search the sky, and she thought she saw an object—something shiny and arching toward the northeast. Was there a tail of fire trailing behind it? She shaded her eyes and focused with every ounce of her attention, but she couldn't see any additional details. The object, whatever it was, simply disappeared from sight.

She hadn't imagined it though. Roxy had danced to the left, tossing her head and neighing in an anxious pitch.

"It's all right girl." She patted the mare's neck and waited for her to settle before continuing on.

Her *abuela* couldn't understand what everyone was so excited about.

"We lived without all of that before." She waved a wrinkled hand toward the sky. "We can live without it again."

"How are you feeling, Abuela?"

"Don't you worry about me, Tanda Kaliska."

Tanda winced at the use of her full name, but her grandmother simply smiled until her eyes crinkled into slits. "It is your nature, I know. But this is not your burden to carry, *nieta*."

"Just doing my job."

"No, you are not. You're trying to do everyone's job, and that is several jobs too many. You are but one woman. Don't forget that."

Tanda didn't have an answer for her *abuela*. The woman was eighty-nine, had shrunk two inches from her full height of five foot, four inches, and couldn't weigh a hundred pounds. Tanda loved her more than life itself. Her grandmother represented everything that was good and right and precious about her family. For Tanda, she seemed to provide a bridge from their collective past to this present world they lived in.

Her mother called them in for a late lunch—thick slices of ham, pan-fried potatoes, and black beans. Her pop spoke of the garden and plans to hunt for quail.

"It's not quail season yet."

"I'm pretty sure it's shoot-anything-you-can season since the Grocery Mart closed."

She didn't know how to respond to that. Had she even seen their game warden since the crash? She didn't think so. Were the hunting laws temporarily suspended? Doubtful.

"Any idea what the falling objects are?" Her pop raised his eyes to hers and waited.

Tanda was somehow touched by that, his seeking answers from her. She'd always felt like a little girl around him, but in this case she was the police chief, and he was worried.

"No idea. I'm not even completely sure they are falling objects." She thought again of the shiny object she might have seen. "I thought I saw something on the ride up here, and earlier—in my office—there was a rumbling that felt like a minor earthquake."

She'd seen a report the month before stating that over seventy earthquakes had occurred in the last year in or near the Alpine area. Most were too small to even be felt. Residents chalked it up to fracking if they thought about it at all.

"Or maybe it is falling objects." She continued to cut her ham, wondering what could be tumbling out of the sky.

"Planes?"

"Maybe. Though I'd think there would be a more obvious crash."

As she was helping to wash the dishes, her mother said, "I want you to go and see your brother."

"Why?"

"Because I'm worried about him."

"Okay." No other reason was really needed. "I can go tomorrow."

"Today, please."

Tanda had meant to go back to work, make sure that everything was running smoothly—which of course it wasn't.

You're trying to do everyone's job, and that is several jobs too many.

"All right. Yeah, of course."

Fortunately Roxy seemed content to turn away from town instead of toward it. Keme lived in a double-wide trailer on the south side of Alpine. She'd tried to convince him to sell the place, move in closer, but he'd refused. Lucy was a professor of literature at Sul Ross. Her specialty was poetry. She looked out of place in the trailer, but she'd never once complained about it. If Keme was there, Lucy was satisfied. They had that kind of love and dedication to one another.

As for her brother, he made his living doing odd jobs for people and raising his children in the old way. Sometimes she thought her niece and nephew appreciated that. Other times she sensed they were embarrassed by it.

They didn't seem to have suffered from their upbringing, but both Akule and Paco had certainly searched for their own path. The oldest, Paco, married a white woman who Tanda had only met once. They now had two children, and the family lived in Dallas.

Akule, Keme's daughter, had tried attending college in Austin, dropped out after a year, bounced around the state for some time, and finally settled down at a job in Alpine. She lived on the east side of town in a small apartment with two other girls. Tanda made a mental note to check on her.

Now it was just Keme and his wife Lucy, living alone and representing an odd amalgamation of the old ways and the new. Tanda supposed that since the crash, they all were.

She tied Roxy's lead rope to a shade tree, promising her treats as soon as they were home. Fortunately, she lived only a few blocks from headquarters and the adjacent horse stables. She could return the horse to its paddock and walk home. She hadn't used her private vehicle since the day before the train wreck, though she did start it one night just to make sure it would work.

"Tanda." Lucy embraced her before she was through the front door. Her sister-in-law was the same height as Tanda but rounder. She'd recently dyed the tips of her hair with turquoise streaks, and she was wearing jeans and a t-shirt that said

Life: It goes on. ~Robert Frost.

"It's good you came. We've been worried about you."

Tanda laughed. "Mom's worried about Keme. Sent me here to check on him."

"It's not me you need to check on." Her brother stood between the kitchen and the living room. He looked solid and healthy and sober.

The fear that she'd been harboring, the fear that he'd relapsed, fled, leaving her feeling simply grateful.

She returned his hug, though it was a bit like being embraced by a giant. They both had their mother's dark hair and brooding Kiowa eyes. Keme had inherited their father's height. All that Tanda was sure she'd inherited from her pop was his Spanish temper.

"Who should I be checking on then?"

"Your government. Make no mistake that they are behind this."

Lucy wagged her hands back and forth in mock frustration. "You talk to him, and maybe he'll stop pestering me with his conspiracy theories."

"Pestering? When Alpine has been scattered away like so much dust, you'll be depending on me to bring you rabbit for dinner."

"Lucy's a better shot than you are, Keme."

"And now you gang up on me." But he smiled, relieving the last of her worry.

Things were good here. She followed him back into the kitchen, and Lucy joined them for a cup of coffee. He'd brought in a butane cookstove and hooked it up on the counter. He noticed her checking to see that he'd properly cracked the window near it and shook his head. "You don't have to worry about us."

"So I see." They spoke of food supplies—both he and their parents had enough to last a month, maybe longer, medication—he and Lucy didn't take any, but they too were concerned about

Abuela's insulin, and neighbors. Two of Keme's had left in the middle of the night.

"Any idea where they went?"

"John was headed south to Big Bend. Said it was the best place to be when society collapses."

"John always was an optimist."

"Franklin was going to try to connect with family in San Angelo."

Tanda studied her coffee, then downed the rest of it, not willing to let the caffeine go to waste. "I hope they make it."

"As do we."

"Any word from Paco or Akule?"

"Paco called before the train crash, but we haven't heard from him since. Akule stopped by yesterday. She seemed okay."

"What about Sul Ross?"

Lucy shrugged. "You know I don't teach summer courses."

"But has the school sent out an email..." Tanda stopped mid-sentence, realizing what a stupid question that was. As if anyone could read their email.

Lucy stood and gathered up the coffee cups. "I am going to tend to my garden. The fresh vegetables will be a nice addition to the canned food. Tanda, you come stay with us if you need to."

"Thank you."

They all knew she wouldn't.

When the front screen door had slapped shut after Lucy, Keme stood. "There's something I want to show you."

Keme's office had always been a strange collection of the old and the new—much like he was. Shelves were filled with water sticks, deer antlers, rocks of various shapes and sizes, and the requisite arrow heads. He'd built a work table across the length of two of the walls, forming an L shape. The workspace was covered with various pieces of computer equipment. Keme was a whiz with electronic things.

"Is any of this working?"

"Not really, not since Tuesday."

She peered at his computer monitor when he turned it on. "How are you on the internet?"

"I'm not."

"But you don't have electricity."

"I have a back-up battery. Every computer geek has one of those." He smiled at her, but there was sadness in it.

Tanda wondered about what he was about to show her.

Wondered if she had the strength to handle one more thing.

"These are screen shots of the windows I had open the day of the crash. When my computer froze, my backup system took screen shots of every open window. It's a program I wrote. Comes in handy more than you'd imagine."

"Okay, but why are you showing me this? I'm not following how it's related to...well, anything."

"Sit down, and let me walk you through it." She sat in his office chair. He snagged a stool from the kitchen and sat down close so that they were shoulder to shoulder and both in front of the computer. "The trains crashed midmorning on Tuesday, right?"

"At 11:02."

"This is a screenshot of the stock exchange at ..." He reached for the mouse, clicked on a box, and enlarged one of the images. "Ten fifty. See this drop? The entire market plummeted, twelve minutes before the train crash. Eighty percent loss. That's unprecedented."

"And you think it's related?"

"I think it's all related."

"Huh." She didn't know what else to say. What could a stock drop have to do with a train crash in west Texas?

He scrolled and clicked on another window. "This is a news station I monitor. Look. This message was displayed at 10:30. That's a full 32 minutes before the Amtrack crash."

Tanda peered at the plain blue screen with *Please Stand By* displayed in a large font. Beneath it was a banner which read, "We are experiencing technical problems at this time."

"Okay. You're saying that something happened—nationally—to the internet."

"I don't know how far the effects reached, but I am ninety percent sure that it started in the cyberworld."

"But the news is...it's just the news."

"It's brought into our homes via satellite. Nearly everything we watch is satellite based now. Local stations barely exist."

"So you think..." She stopped, shook her head. "What are you suggesting, Keme?

"That everything's down."

"Here?"

"Everywhere." He leaned forward and tapped the computer screen. "Everything we depend on in modern society—from stock markets to news to communication—it's all down."

Her heart beat faster and her mind scrambled to catch up, but she couldn't make the pieces fit together. This event—whatever it was—had all started Tuesday morning. It had started, according to Keme's screenshots, before they'd even been aware. "The train crash..."

"Trains depend on computer guidance to determine their speed and warn them of approaching vehicles."

"Only it didn't."

"It couldn't if everything had gone off-line."

Tanda frowned at the screen. Somehow, she'd assumed that whatever was happening was limited to their area, that soon someone would come riding in or helicoptering in, apologizing for their tardiness, and explaining that they had come to get Alpine up and running again. "You think everything's down?"

"Everything."

"Like..."

"Like, everything. Look at this." He pulled up a third and final screen. "This was trending on Twitter, less than an hour before the crash. I clicked on it at..." He checked the time stamp on the screen. "Fourteen minutes after ten."

"What am I looking at?"

"Video footage of a plane crash."

"What?" She leaned closer and made out the image of a woman—frightened, about to die. Behind her were other passengers who understood that the end had come. It was a terrifying tableau. It was unconscionable for this to be floating around on social media, though she supposed that all of those platforms were now also down. "Who is this?"

"Some lady flying a direct flight from London to Austin."

"And her plane crashed?"

"Over the Atlantic. They were a couple hours into the flight. She was live-streaming and then it just...it just stopped."

Tanda sat back in her chair, spun it around so that she was staring at the rain sticks and rocks...things that seemed infinitely more real than the images on Keme's screen.

Finally, she looked at her brother. "I don't know what any of that means."

"I don't think anyone does." He clicked off the computer monitor.

"Explain to me how that's working."

"Back-up battery which is being charged by our generator." When she only stared at him, he said, "We have a generator. Don't you?"

"I'm in an apartment, Keme. No, I don't have a generator."

"How's that working out for you?"

"It's fine."

"Really? Because you can come stay out here. We have plenty of room."

"I like being near work."

"Okay."

She stood, walked through the trailer as if she were passing through a murky dream. Keme followed her out the front door. She waved goodbye to Lucy who was still working the garden, then untethered her horse.

"Cops on horses." Keme gave the horse a scratch on the forehead, laughed when Roxy nodded appreciatively. "It really is the end of the world."

But Tanda wasn't ready to laugh about their situation, not after all that he'd just shown her. She stood next to her horse. Roxy pulled against the reins, ready to go, to be home—fed and stabled.

"What you showed me, it proves that it's not just Alpine that's unplugged. It's everyone."

"I think so, yeah."

"Which means no one is coming to help us."

"I wouldn't expect the cavalry. Not for a long time anyway."

She hesitated, thought of the way her pop had looked at her, and pushed through with the question. "The earthquakes, or crashes, or whatever...are those related too?"

"They would have to be."

"And your conspiracy theory?"

He looked as if he wouldn't answer that particular question, studied her a moment, and then asked a question of his own. "What could have caused something of this magnitude?"

"I don't know." Her heart rate again accelerated. "Terrorism?"

"If you're asking me, and I'm a computer geek, Tanda, not an analyst, but it seems to me that it would have to be one of three things." He ticked him off on his fingers. "Domestic terrorism..."

"An attack from within, against our infrastructure."

"International terrorism."

"An attack from without, which could mean we're at war."

"Or a natural disaster."

She thought about what Logan had said about the cars working. "Not a solar flare."

"No, not that."

"What else is there?"

Keme shrugged, stepped back from her horse. "I've blown your mind enough for one afternoon. We'll talk about it next time."

She hugged him once more, swung up into her saddle and made her way home. Tired as she was, she couldn't sleep that night. Every time she'd drop off, she'd see the image of the woman's face, terrified as her plane plummeted toward the cold waters of the Atlantic. Tanda tossed and turned, and finally gave up the fight and threw back her covers.

She made a cup of herbal tea, grateful that her stove was gas powered, and even tried reading an old Elmer Kelton novel on her e-reader. Then she realized that her e-reader wouldn't be working much longer, so she clicked it off and dressed for work. She was at her desk before six a.m.

There wasn't much to do—no paper work or reports to file since the computer system was down. She'd taken to keeping notes in an old log book that the chief before her had used. Even so, there wasn't much to log. People were behaving themselves, for now. If they were to see what was on Keme's computer, she wasn't sure how they'd react.

Would they panic?

Would they turn on one another?

This was Alpine though. Sure, there was tension between the hippy art community and the old-time ranchers, but when times were hard, they pulled together. At least they had in the past.

"Chief. I think you're going to want to see this."

Conor sounded more amused than worried. She took the time to close the log book and place it in her bottom drawer, then joined him at the front window.

"That your doctor?"

"Yup."

"I guess he's bringing his dog to work."

"I guess he is."

Chapter 7

MILES STEPPED INTO THE police station, surprised that there were only two people there—Chief Lopez and a young man who looked barely old enough to carry a gun.

The young man behind the desk stood and offered his hand. "Conor Johnson. You must be Doc Turner. Good to meet you."

Miles shook his hand, his gaze travelling from the young officer to the neatly organized workspace to Tanda Lopez.

"Let's step into my office."

He signaled to Zeus to stay, but Chief Lopez only smiled. "Bring him with you. We're patrolling on horses. Our town doctor might as well have a canine assistant."

It had been a long time since he'd stepped inside anything resembling a professional building. As he followed Chief Lopez into her office, his mind wanted to flip back to the last time he was in a police station, but he shut that door in his mind firmly.

"Coffee?" Chief Lopez held up a thermos. "I make it at home on my gas stove."

"I'd love some." His voice was gravelly. He cleared it, then tried again. "Thank you."

He hooked a thumb back toward the front desk. "Are you sure he's old enough to be an officer?"

"Yeah. I checked him out before I hired him."

She poured him a mug full of steaming coffee, then left the office and came back with a bowl of water for Zeus. The dog looked to Miles for permission.

"Go ahead," Miles said.

Zeus didn't have to be told twice. He lapped up the water, then flopped onto the floor, legs spread out in front of him.

"Your dog still alive?"

"I think so."

The coffee was exactly what he needed. He savored it, not anxious to begin this conversation now that he was sitting across from Chief Lopez.

She looked out the window as if she were searching for something, then turned her attention back to him. "I hope you're here because you've had a change of heart."

"I'm not sure." He stared into the coffee. "But after your visit, well...let's just say my need-to-know was piqued. Any updates?"

"None."

"I saw the trains."

"Yeah. That's a real mess."

"Why hasn't it been cleaned up?"

"We don't have the kind of heavy machinery needed to move those freight cars. Usually the FRA—"

"Who?"

"Federal Railroad Administration. Usually, they'd have investigators on site within hours. Obviously, in a standard emergency situation, they don't want the scene messed with—not that we've had a train crash in Alpine before, but we've been trained for what we're expected to do should one occur."

"Your training is to do what?"

"Treat injuries. If anything's on fire, put it out. That's pretty much it. The FRA reaches out to contractors who come and clean it up."

"But you haven't heard from them?"

"Nope."

"And the other stuff—phones, electric, water..."

Tanda tapped the thermos. "We're getting by, but yes...everything's still out, and the situation becomes a little more challenging every day."

"Any idea what's caused it all?"

She shifted in her chair and her eyes darted to a family picture on her desk. "There are a few theories, but those are pretty preliminary. I'm not comfortable sharing them at this point."

"Fair enough." As a physician, he didn't always tell a patient his immediate theories. He waited until testing confirmed what he suspected was wrong.

"I'm going to be honest with you, Dr. Turner."

"Miles." He didn't know why he said that. He wasn't inviting familiarity, but it felt safer than her reminding him that he was a doctor with every greeting. Then again, he was here to do that very thing, so what was the point in hiding from it? "Just...Miles is fine."

"Okay, and please call me Tanda." She waited for him to nod. "I want to say, up front, that I'm sorry about your wife and daughter."

She watched him, silently—waiting. She let him process the words, push back the pain.

"How do you know about that?"

Instead of answering, she placed both her hands on the table—one on top of the other. He almost laughed that he'd first wondered if she was an alcoholic. She was one of the calmest persons he'd ever been around. Calm and...intentional, that was the word he was looking for.

"I can understand why a person would want to just...go off the grid. But in this case, we need each other."

Miles wasn't sure about that. Did he need these people? He'd been doing fine in his cabin on Old Ranch Road. He and Zeus were pretty self-sufficient. Not completely though, and that was part of the reason he'd decided to come to town.

"The stores are still closed?"

"They are."

"But you have some supplies."

"Yes. We have emergency supplies. Since this is still largely a farming and ranching town, a portion of those supplies includes seed and feed."

"I'll need chicken feed. Fifty pounds once a month. And dog food."

Zeus whimpered in his sleep.

"We can do that."

"You're sure?"

"I'll find you what you need, Miles. I don't make a promise unless I'm sure I can keep it."

He could see that was true. "I guess I'll take your word then. I remember a medical center outside of town. Is that where you want me?"

"Alpine has a regional medical center on 118. I've checked on them—there are only a few patients at the moment, and there are nurses still showing up for work."

"No doctors?"

"No. Doc Fielder was the only one in town when the crash happened."

He thought leaving only one physician in town had been a bit short-sighted, but then no one could have envisioned their current situation.

"I'd rather have you here, closer to the center of town, where people can get to you more easily."

There was something different about Tanda Lopez. She was certainly unlike any cop he'd ever met. Her manner was all business, but her eyes were *soulful*. It was a ridiculous thought, but that was what came to mind.

"I'll work three days a week. That's the most I can give you."

"We'll take it, and thank you."

"Where is—"

"Dr. Fielder's office is a few buildings down the street."

"He died...of a heart attack?"

"Yes."

"Okay." He stood and whistled for Zeus, who stretched then clambered rather ungracefully to his feet.

"I guess you walked this morning."

"I did."

"You have a Jeep..."

"Yes, but I figured I should save the gas."

She nodded in approval. "Do you need a horse?"

He laughed, and wasn't that a foreign sound to his ears. "There's a job perk I've never been offered, but no, thank you. We'll walk."

Tanda held out her hand and he shook it. "I imagine you never expected to work for chicken feed either, but we are where we find ourselves."

We are where we find ourselves.

That simple statement followed him as she walked with him out into a glorious June morning. Sunlight splattered across the street, the summer air was pleasantly cool, and a mourning dove called from its perch on a streetlight that no longer worked.

He thought of his wife and daughter.

Thought of the world he'd left—one that confused and devastated him.

Thought of the refuge he'd created on Old Ranch Road.

That refuge had been an illusion. It seemed there was no where he could go, no place remote enough that he could hide, no place where the troubles of the world wouldn't find him.

Chapter 8

Tanda left Dr. Miles Turner in the competent hands of Anita Sanchez. Anita had been Dr. Fielder's assistant for the last twenty years. She was slim, Hispanic, and somewhat bossy. She could answer more questions about the community's medical needs than Tanda could. Tanda looked back once before heading out onto the street. Anita was reaching down to scratch Zeus between the ears. Miles stood in the middle of the room, eyes locked on something far away.

Thinking of his wife and daughter, perhaps.

The pain on his face when she'd offered her condolences had made her want to pull back the words, but she didn't like knowing something about a person that they weren't aware she knew. It set an artificial tone to every conversation. Better to put it out in the open. At least she hoped it was better.

Back at the station, Conor had been replaced by their receptionist, Edna. She had recently celebrated her fifty-fifth birthday, refused to put up with any type of nonsense, and was not intimidated by anyone or anything. She somehow brought a feeling of business-as-usual to the office. When Edna was at the desk, everyone knew that things were as they should be.

Unfortunately, the peace of the morning didn't last.

At 9:25, a young boy sprinted to their office to report shots fired. By the time Tanda and Makowski followed him to the residence in question, the situation had escalated. Mrs. Benson's dog had trampled Mr. Avery's vegetable garden. Mr. Avery was threatening to shoot the pooch, and Mrs. Benson was having none of it. Tanda was afraid she was going to have to arrest them both, and she really didn't want to take them back to a jail cell with no air conditioning.

It took thirty minutes of negotiation, but Mrs. Benson finally agreed not to let Skipper out the front door unattended, and Mr. Avery agreed to put up his shotgun.

The next call didn't have such a happy ending.

Since it was, indeed, a call, it could be one of only a few people. There were probably less than twelve folks in town who still had a land line.

Edna took down the information and now stood at the door to Tanda's office, reading what she'd written. "Simon Grant died during the night. His granddaughter went to check on him and found the body. She's hysterical and insisting we send the ambulance over to pick him up."

"I'll take care of it, Chief." Regina Grant had just come on duty. "Want me to transport him to the morgue?"

"No. Walk down to the fire house and ask the EMPs to pick him up in an ambulance." The last thing they needed was for people to see them slinging corpses over the back of a horse. "Then go on over to his home and see if there's anything else the family needs."

"You've got it." Regina had joined the department with a bad attitude and three years of less-than-stellar law enforcement experience with the Houston PD. It had taken her a year to unlearn the bad lessons of her previous position, and another year to drop the chip from her shoulder. She still took herself a bit too seriously, but overall, Tanda thought that she had the potential to be a good officer.

It bothered Tanda to know that the number of civilian deaths continued to increase. Their older population was vulnerable to heat strokes as well as dangerous repercussions from lack of medication. What could they do to avoid it? Her mind flashed to her *abuela*. She'd purchased her monthly supply of insulin the day before the crash, and her parents were keeping it cold by plugging a small refrigerator into their generator.

What would happen to those people who had planned to fill their prescriptions this week? There wasn't anything they could do. Was there? She'd ask Miles. Maybe they should start wellness checks on the older residents. But they were already spread thin with the reduction in EMP staff. There still hadn't been a word from the people who had gone out the week before, gone with an ambulance full of injured to Fort Stockton. Had they even arrived? Had they been unable to come back?

They might be able to do something like a neighborhood watch group—a check on your neighbor group. She started to pull out her phone to tap on NOTES, but charging the phone every day probably wasn't the best use of her time or generator power. She walked around to her desk, opened the top drawer and pulled out a small pocket notepad. Turning the cover back, she started a list.

The mayor had another meeting scheduled for the next day and the first public meeting scheduled for Wednesday. They needed to be ahead of as many of the upcoming problems as they could. Catching up was simply too hard.

The questions piled on top of Tanda until she thought the weight would crush her. She grabbed her sunglasses and hat. "Going to patrol the business section. I'll be back in twenty."

Edna waved and promised, "We'll send up a flare if we need you."

The day had grown warmer. She purposely walked in the opposite direction of Dr. Fielder's office. She didn't want Miles to think she was checking up on him. Instead, she headed to the old business sectioned, circled the block, and then started back toward headquarters via a different side street.

A shrill scream caused her to stop in the middle of the sidewalk and pivot back the way she'd come. The screaming intensified. A woman's voice for certain.

Tanda broke into a run.

She arrived in time to see a twenty-something-year-old repeat offender attempting to yank a purse from a young mom's hands. The mom was holding her baby in one arm and trying to shake off the thief with the other. A small dog darted back and forth in the grass, barking incessantly. No one was minding the little terrier. The woman and thief stood on the porch, playing tug-of-war with her purse.

Owen Bradley—his name came to her in a flash—gave the strap one mighty yank, ripped it from the woman's arms, and took off at a sprint. He turned in the direction of Tanda, who had her service revolver drawn.

She shouted, "Stop, drop the purse, and put your hands in the air."

Owen skidded to a stop, tossed her a wild look, and tore off in the opposite direction. The combination of exhaustion, frustration, and outrage had Tanda sighting him down the barrel of her Glock.

She almost did it.

She almost pulled the trigger.

Then the woman's baby began to cry, pulling Tanda back to her senses. She holstered her weapon and took off after Owen. He was more than ten years younger, but he wasn't exactly a specimen of health. Methamphetamines and weed had stolen that from him. She caught him in the next block, slammed him to the pavement, and cuffed him.

"What did you go and do that for, Owen?"

"I didn't do nothing. Get off of me."

She frog-marched him back to the scene of the crime, tossed the purse to the woman whose baby was still crying, and told her that Officer Grant would be by with a complaint form later in the day.

"Where you taking me?" Owen sputtered.

"To jail. That's where we put offenders."

"But I heard there weren't no judges."

"The law's still the law, Owen. You can't just go around robbing people and expect to get away with it."

"Who said I robbed anybody?"

She didn't bother arguing. She was starting to regret her evening before—the tossing and the tea and the Elmer Kelton book. She was starting to believe her *abuela* was right about her attempting to do too much. She'd put Owen into a cell and decide what to do with him later. She'd finish her shift, and after that she planned to sleep for the next twelve hours.

It wasn't quite that simple.

Someone cooking on a BBQ pit dropped a coal onto the ground, starting a grass fire that took the joint effort of the fire department and police department to put out.

They used shovels and dirt and blankets to beat the flames into submission. Why weren't they using water? They still had water the last time she checked. Before she could ask Chief Peters, she was called out to a domestic dispute, and then a break-in at Sam's Bait and More shop.

She made it back to her office in time to read a note from Ben Cason. The mayor's meeting had been moved up. Tanda had twenty minutes to clean up, change her soot-covered, sweat-stained uniform, and walk to city hall.

Something told her they'd entered a new phase of whatever *this* was. She only wished they had someone leading them besides Melinda Stone.

Chapter 9

"**S**HE HAS ONE IN the jail—a tweeker named Owen."

"What does she plan to do with him?"

"No idea."

Melinda Stone stood at the windows, staring down at the people scurrying around like little ants. The first sign of trouble and people went into a panic. It had been less than a week and already law and order had begun to break down. It was a pity she wasn't in charge of the police department.

Though, actually, as mayor—she kind of was.

"Anything else?"

"No. Other than she seems pretty cozy with the new doc."

"Is that so?" Something to file away for a rainy day. A widowed doctor and a lonely police chief...that could be made to look like quite the scandal.

"And the fire?" She'd been able to see the flames from her office window.

"Out. Dixie Peters left two of her people on sight to watch for flare ups."

Dixie Peters. There was another ineffective woman in a position of leadership. Most days, Melinda felt as if she was the only one of her gender able to cope with the requirements of her job.

"Did you relocate the bottled water to my store room?"

"Ten cases, like you asked."

"I suppose that will do for now." She couldn't be expected to drink tap water, and since it seemed all deliveries were halted it was a matter of each person fending for herself.

"The problem with a disaster is that too many people feel like they need to be in charge. I'll clear that up at tonight's meeting. Then on Wednesday we'll inform the citizens of Alpine what will be expected from them. Or maybe..."

She almost laughed. It wasn't funny. She knew that, but really...this was just a test of some sort. People had such a tendency to panic, like when that doctor had died. He'd been old. She was surprised he'd survived as long as he did. But did "the people" see it that way?

No.

Her office had been filled with citizens demanding to know what she was going to do. It was a good thing she'd instructed Ben Cason to keep a file on every high-profile person who moved into the area. Miles Turner definitely fit that description. If it weren't for her, he'd still be up in his cabin, pining away over some distant tragedy.

As for the *event* or *collapse* or whatever people were calling it, she wasn't worried. It would pass the same way the 9-11 crisis and the Covid pandemic had passed. If only people would calm down. One week in and she was already exhausted. It was all she could do not to climb into her Tesla and head over to Fort Stockton or San Antonio.

A drive out of town would probably do her good. She could be the one to bring back information.

But she couldn't trust these vipers three hours on their own, let alone an entire day or two.

"Maybe, at the town meeting, I'll let them see just how incompetent their leaders are. Give Mullins and Peters and Garcia...give Tanda Lopez a few minutes with a microphone and the town will come begging for me to institute martial law." She sat up straighter, touched each of her fingers to her thumb—forward then back again. It was something a private yoga instructor had said would strengthen her aura. "Yes. I think it will be better coming from the people. Of course, if you were to put the suggestion in the right places..."

"Consider it done."

"Good!" She clapped her hands. "And trust me, I won't forget how helpful you've been."

Chapter 10

MILES HAD NO INTENTION of going to the public meeting scheduled for Wednesday evening. He'd spent the last two nights on a cot in his office, and he was looking forward to being back at his cabin, to being alone and away from people.

It wasn't that the good folks of Alpine were that difficult to be around. They were the same as people anywhere—some were hardworking, others a bit lazy. Old and young. Artist and rancher. It's what had drawn him to the medical field—the great hodgepodge of human life. He'd once enjoyed that aspect of his work. Now that same assortment of folks wore him down. He supposed he had become used to his own company—his and his dog's. If he were honest, that trend had begun before he'd moved to Alpine. It was why he'd moved to Alpine. People had become too much, interaction taxing, and socializing downright painful.

"You going to the meeting, Doc?" Anita stood in his doorway, clipboard in hand.

Anita always had her clipboard in hand. She ran a tight ship, and he was grateful for her efficiency. Either Doc Fielder had trained her right, or she'd kept him straight much as she was keeping Miles straight now.

"Thought I'd skip it. Zeus and I are headed home tonight."

"You should go." Anita was only forty-eight years old, but her gaze held pools of wisdom.

Viejo y sabio.

Old and wise.

Still, he really wanted to go home. He dropped his stethoscope into his medical bag—yes, he had a medical bag. Anita had found Fielder's old brown leather one in a closet. She had dusted it off, filled it with supplies he might need for a medical emergency, and left it on the middle of his desk.

"You can stay here tonight and walk home in the morning. The mornings are cooler. It'll be better for your dog."

Zeus, the traitor, wagged his tail in agreement.

"Tell me you aren't afraid the meeting will end in a fistfight or, even worse, shots fired." He meant it as a joke. In the last three days he'd treated a broken arm, several cases of allergies, and quite a bit of heat exhaustion. No physical altercations. No gunshot wounds.

"It might," she said with a straight face, and then she was gone.

Miles sank into his chair and stared at Zeus.

He'd rather be home, but a part of him was curious as to how the power vacuum in their little town was being filled.

With a sigh, he stood and walked to his small but private bathroom. There was no shower, but since water was so limited it was just as well that he wasn't tempted to waste it on five minutes under a hot stream. He reminded himself it would be a cold stream of water. Shrugging, he measured out half a cup from the jug Anita had placed there, wet a washcloth, and cleaned up as best he could. His choice of clothing was a clean pair of scrubs or the shirt and jeans he'd worn to town on Monday morning. He chose the jeans and t-shirt.

Whistling once at Zeus, he walked to the front door of the clinic, surprised to see so many people out on the streets. They were all walking toward the town's pavilion, where the meeting was to be held. The pavilion was situated next to the county courthouse. Miles joined the crowd, responding with a nod to the greetings tossed his way. He didn't speak to anyone directly until a little girl of six threw herself at his legs, encircling them with her good arm and giving him a hug.

Then she proudly raised her new cast. "I've been coloring. See?"

"Nicely done. And you've been keeping it in the sling, like we talked about?"

She carefully pulled the Miss Kitty sling back over the cast. "Most of the time. I only take it off to show people my coloring."

Bethany's parents tossed him an appreciative smile as they all turned the corner toward the pavilion.

Miles wasn't sure what he'd expected, but it wasn't this. Closest to the pavilion were mostly older residents. They were seated in lawn chairs, some even sporting a cooler from which they pulled warm drinks. Ice had run out days ago.

Behind the seniors were families—some on picnic blankets, most with strollers, all with children running back and forth in games of tag and hide-n-seek and Marco Polo. On the outer edges of those assembled lurked the teenagers. Miles hadn't realized there were so many. Looking closer, he saw that quite a few wore Sul Ross t-shirts. So, teens and college students.

He'd barely given the campus a thought since arriving in town a year ago. It seemed inconceivable that students were still attending classes. So what were they doing? Who was looking after them? Did then even need looking after? They were, after all, adults. He thought of his first year at college and grimaced. It was something he should bring up with Tanda.

Some of the teens sat astride bikes.

A few were playing catch or frisbee.

Most stood staring at the stage, a look of glum acceptance on their faces. They'd been expecting a global disaster since they watched their first dystopian movie—*Divergent* or *Hunger Games* or *District 9*. The expressions on their faces said they'd known it was coming, but why did it have to come when the freedom of adulthood was just within sight?

Or maybe they were simply hot and tired like everyone else.

There was another group consisting of ranchers—skin dark and resembling leather. Most were scrawny and muscular with eyes cautiously studying the folks around them.

Off to the left was a final group. Their clothing was trendy, their haircuts styled to look mussed and carefree. They looked—different. Out of place even. Definitely uncomfortable. So this was the famous artist community he'd been hearing about. Miles was beginning to wish he'd brought a lawn chair. The night's events could turn into quite the show.

Mayor Stone spoke first. She'd dressed as if she planned to attend a corporate business meeting—designer suit, heels, lots of jewelry and lipstick a tad too bright. She spoke into a microphone that was hooked up to a small amplifier.

Miles had no problem hearing her, as the crowd immediately quieted. She began by assuring them that everything was under control and pivoted into reminding them of the upcoming elections the following May.

Several folks began to grumble, and one shouted out, "If we're all still here next year."

Stone gave him a pointed stare and an over-wide smile. "And now I'll hand the microphone over to our fire chief, Dixie Peters."

The woman who took the microphone wore khaki pants and a polo shirt. She was neither thin nor heavy, and she looked rather young to be in charge of a fire department. Her blonde hair was pulled back from her face, and her expression was grim.

"As you all know, we've had several small fires since the day of the collapse."

"We don't even know what that means. What collapsed?" This from an old farmer holding a Stetson.

"I'll leave that to Mr. Mullins to explain since he's in charge of public works. Suffice it to say that we need you to be extra vigilant when burning candles, using generators, and especially while using propane cooking stoves. It's safest to do so outside. If you must use one inside, be sure the window nearest to the stove is left open."

"All my windows are open since the electricity went out," an old woman up front shouted. "Not that it helps cool down my place any."

The grumbling rose again, but Peters held up a hand and raised her voice over the crowd. "My department has been placing percussion instruments that we borrowed from the high school in every neighborhood. We've also posted a map of those locations on the courthouse door to my right. Be sure that you familiarize yourself with it."

A young man with three small children stood, "Let me get this straight. I'm supposed to run to the corner and bang a snare drum if my house catches on fire?"

"Yes, sir, you are. My crew can't be at every spot in this town at every moment, and as you've noticed 9-1-1 no longer works. Cymbals, drums, gongs—we used whatever instruments make the loudest sound. Also, you should respond if you hear anyone else's instrument. Please caution your children that these are not toys."

She paused, as if trying to decide whether to voice the next thought, then pushed on. "If we're going to get through this, we'll do so by depending on each other."

Miles noticed that while a few folks continued to grumble, most nodded their head in approval. Peters was using whatever was at her disposal to keep the community safe, and that didn't go unnoticed.

Emmanuel Garcia, the county health coordinator was middle-aged and looked completely out of his element. He rubbed the palms of his hands against his jeans before accepting the microphone. "We haven't received any county health information from outside our area. There's no indication that this is a health crisis, although it certainly could become one. Later this week, I'll be meeting with our new doctor—"

Everyone turned to look at Miles. Unsure what else to do, he offered a small wave.

"We'll come up with a plan for getting you what medication and food supplies you need. County reserves also include a good supply of crop seeds as well as some feed for the livestock. The distribution of those goods will be done in an orderly and fair manner." Garcia practically threw the microphone at the next guy and scampered off the stage before anyone could ask a question.

Ron Mullins was the director of public works. He was balding with something of a paunch, but his gaze was steady and he didn't shy away from speaking to the group. "Jackson, you asked what collapsed. Our infrastructure did. I can't tell you what caused it so I don't know how long it will be down. In fact, there isn't a lot I can say that you haven't figured out for yourself. All communications and power are no longer working."

"Why doesn't my water work?" This from an elderly woman with wispy white hair.

"Our water comes from a well system. The pumps as well as the lift stations require electricity. We recently had a new back-up system installed. Generators that were guaranteed to provide power in case of a temporary outage, but this..." He paused, looked out past the crowd, and then brought his attention back to them.

"The generators are out of fuel. No generator, no power to run the pumps. That's why your water doesn't work, Mrs. Simpson."

A tall, burly man wearing a baseball cap stood and hitched up his pants. "There's fuel at the gas stations."

"But there's no electricity to pump it up and out of those tanks."

"It's in the ground though. If we could break through into the tank, we could siphon it out."

"You're not punching a hole in my tanks." A woman whose skin was as weathered as an old saddle stood, shaking her head. "This thing won't last forever. When it's over, I need those pumps to work and they won't if you punch a damn hole in them."

The crowd was silent for a moment as everyone's thoughts turned to that bright thought—*this thing won't last forever*.

Mullins ran a hand over the top of his head. "I think county funds could be used for the repairs, if and when this is over. I'll meet with our city attorney and get back to both of you, but it's a good idea, Tate."

Mullins seemed to search the crowd. Shaking his head, he handed the microphone to Tanda. Miles had barely spoken to the police chief since coming to town. He had the distinct impression that she was giving him space, as if afraid he might startle and scamper away.

Like the first time he'd seen her, he was impressed by her steadiness, the calmness in those dark brown eyes. He noticed that the various conversations around him ceased when she cleared her throat.

"I don't have much to add to what the others have said, but I would like to emphasize that the laws of our community still stand. We will not tolerate theft, burglary, assault, drug possession, or any other type of nefarious behavior." She somehow delivered the last two words with a smile, causing the people around Miles to chuckle and nod in agreement.

"I do not want to put people in a jail cell. Like your homes, it's quite uncomfortable during midday. Unlike your homes, there are no windows in the cells that open to provide any sort of breeze." Now the crowd was perfectly silent, waiting. "That won't stop me from incarcerating people who threaten the welfare of others."

More nods of agreement.

"I don't know what this thing that has happened to us is, and to tell you the truth, it scares me. I'm frightened for my *abuela*, for our citizens..." She hesitated, staring at the floor of the gazebo for a moment. When she'd gained control of her emotions she look up again, her eyes scanning the crowd and confidence returning to her voice.

"We have good people here in Alpine, and I do honestly believe that we can get through today and tomorrow and the day after that...if we do so together. Help your neighbor. Share what you have. Sign up on one of the advisory boards or work teams." She waved back toward the courthouse where a table was set up. Three teenagers standing behind the table all offered a small wave. "I shudder to think what things are like in Fort Stockton or El Paso or New York—and before you ask, no, I do not know if it extends that far. It makes sense that it would, since we haven't heard from anyone."

"What about the teams we sent out to Fort Davis, Marathon, and Marfa?" This from Tate, the man who'd suggested puncturing the fuel tanks.

"They haven't returned, and we've heard nothing. Until we do have more information, it's critical that we pull together, share what we have, and help our neighbors."

The reality of what they were facing seemed to fall on them all in that moment. It felt heavy and frightening and dangerous. Miles thought the meeting would end there, with every one having had their eyes opened, with any foolishly optimistic ideas having been stripped away. But it didn't.

Someone from the art group stood and began shouting.

"Do you honestly expect someone on that side of town to help someone on our side?" The man gestured toward the farmers who stood as a single unit. "They'd sooner see us starve than offer something out of their gardens. So we won't be sharing what we have because it's our private property. This is still the United State of America, and we still have constitutional rights..."

"Your kind is always going on about constitutional rights." Jackson pushed his hat down more firmly on his head. "Why don't you shut your mouth for once and consider what's good for the group."

The middle-aged man with long hair and a scraggly beard who had started the verbal skirmish answered with an upraised middle finger.

And that was all it took.

His words were drowned out by others around him—some apparently agreeing, others openly confronting the man.

Miles didn't see who threw the first punch. Could have been the man shaped like a bull standing in the space between the art community and the ranchers. Maybe it was one of the young men who'd just realized his life had changed irrevocably. Could have even been one of the artists.

It quickly turned into a melee.

One of the officers started blowing a whistle. The mayor attempted to shout over the group with the microphone. Tanda waded into the crowd. None of that helped.

The frustration of the previous week and the fear of the days ahead fueled tempers that were stretched thin. Families with children were trying to back out of the worst of it. The group of teens and college students were looking on in amazement, unsure how to respond to this sudden lack of control on the part of the adults who were in charge. But in the midst, throwing punches right and left, were farmers and blue-collar workers, painters and poets. The two sides of Alpine clashed much as the trains had a week earlier.

It might have continued that way until one or the other side won, until they were a bloodied, battered mass of humanity. But a high-pitched whining sound caught everyone's attention. Glancing up, Miles saw a fiery object streaking across the sky, looking as if it was coming straight for them. Maybe a plane or a rocket or...

His mind went blank.

What could be streaking across their sky?

A meteor?

He didn't have much time to ponder it though. A high-pitched sound filled the air, causing young children near him to clap their hands over their ears. The angry screams of a moment before changed to frightened cries. Folks started snatching up babies and toddlers and even old people. Wild-eyed and scared, they took off in a dozen different directions—the old fight or flight instinct now firmly in control.

There was no fighting whatever this was.

So they fled—or attempted to.

A few tripped, lay on the ground with their arms over their head, and still the noise from the thing falling out of the sky grew louder.

Miles rushed over to help an older woman who was clinging to her walker and attempting to push it over a blanket that had been left on the ground. He looked up in time to see Tanda scooping up a little girl under one arm and a frightened dog under the other.

She turned toward him and their eyes locked.

And he realized that they were in this together—regardless of what *this* was. He wouldn't have called the pull between them attraction or romantic. It was more fundamental than that.

Maybe fate.

Maybe destiny.

And then the thing, whatever it was, catapulted past them and seconds later it crashed, causing the ground to shake and a loud rumble to fill the air.

Chapter 11

A FTER THE OBJECT FELL from the sky, Tanda had no trouble being heard. Folks were staring at one another, then looking up, looking into the distance, looking back at her—everyone frozen in place. Tanda strode to the gazebo and jerked the microphone out of the mayor's hand.

"Officers Grant and Makowski are going to ride north and find out what that was. Officers Rodriguez and Johnson will be stationed at the north and south ends of this block to ensure that you all leave in an orderly fashion. We will send word through your neighborhood coordinators as well as post it on the courthouse door. If we need you, we will call you. Until then, I want you to return to your homes. If you require medical attention, Dr. Turner will be waiting next to the sign-up table."

It wasn't the note she'd hoped to end the meeting on, but at least people had stopped punching one another. Her ears felt as if they were plugged. She opened her jaw wide, yawned, and the pressure in her ears popped. Her hands were shaking as she handed the microphone back to Stone and walked away.

Grant and Makowski met her behind the stage, both leading their horses, their expressions grim but determined.

"Seemed to land north-northwest, chief. Maybe past the 06 Ranch." Grant looked at Makowski for confirmation.

Makowski simply shrugged. "I was in the middle of something at the moment."

And that was when Tanda noticed the skin around his left eye swelling.

"If that punch was directed at you, I'll arrest whoever was stupid enough to hit one of my officers."

Makowski waved away the idea. "Chalk it up to being in the wrong place at the wrong time."

"Are you able to ride?"

"Sure."

"Okay. Take the horses out via 118. Try to get close enough to see what it was, but do not leave the city limits."

Grant hoisted herself up into her saddle. "Shouldn't we keep riding until we find it? If it was a plane there could be people who need help."

"It wasn't a plane, and if it was, no one could have survived that kind of crash." Tanda shook her head. "We still don't understand what has happened, what is happening, but everyone who has left this town has not come back. I need you two to come back."

Makowski and Grant exchanged a look, then both nodded in agreement. Makowski swung up into the saddle, a move that looked oddly natural despite his size and weight. The horses took off at a brisk walk, breaking into a trot when they reached the outer edge of the group.

Dixie pushed her way through the crowd. "I could take one of the fire trucks out..."

"No. Better to save whatever fuel you have for an Alpine emergency—one where you could do some good. Whatever happened out there..." She wiped at the sweat pooling across her forehead. "Without water pressure you couldn't put out a fire of that size."

Dixie nodded in agreement. "I'll have a team on stand-by if you need us."

"Do all of your people have first aid training?"

"Yeah. They all recertified earlier this year."

"Send a couple over to help Miles."

When she looked toward the sign-up table, she wasn't too surprised to see Logan Wright standing next to the doctor. There were at least two dozen people waiting to be treated.

"That was fun. Nothing like fireworks at the end of a town meeting." The mayor's voice was oddly chirpy. "And the commotion before the flaming thing reminded me of a brawl at a football game."

"This isn't a game."

"Of course it's not, but people are hot-headed at times—especially your rancher people."

"*My* rancher people?"

"They've always had a superior attitude toward the art community. Rather than thanking them for bringing tourist dollars to our area, they antagonize them."

"It was a man from the artist community who started that entire exchange—"

Stone cut her off with a shake of her head. The mayor looked down and focused on straightening the hem of her jacket. How could she even stand wearing a jacket in this heat?

Finally, Stone said, "Gonzo needed to burn off some frustration is all. Your people took it too far."

Tanda didn't know how to answer that. But she thought that if people had anything they needed to burn off there were more productive ways to do so than shouting insults or slamming their fist into someone's face.

She walked away as the mayor turned her attention to Ron Mullins, criticizing him for "scaring the people." To her surprise, Ron was standing up to her, or so it sounded from the little she heard.

Ninety minutes later, Tanda, Miles, and Logan were the only ones left under the gazebo. Grant and Makowski had returned—there were no flames to the north. Whatever had crash landed didn't appear to be on fire. The actual crash site was too far north to be seen from the town's city limit, but flames would have been visible for miles.

The sun had set, but it wasn't yet dark.

A cool breeze ruffled the leaves in the trees.

Tanda felt as if she could sleep, sitting on the top step with her back braced against the gazebo's structure. "What's the final tally?"

"Three people needed butterfly stitches, one person twisted his ankle, and another was experiencing chest pains." Miles leaned forward and scratched Zeus between the ears. "I have to say, it was nice to have the help of the town vet."

"My side of the table wasn't so bad. I treated a couple of black eyes that could have used ice, which we don't have. Plus, a dog that was inadvertently stepped on—he's going to be fine—and a young man with a busted lip." Logan shook his head in mock disbelief. "Vets administering aid to people—I've become an apocalyptic stereotype."

"My department is riding horses."

"I sleep on a cot in my office—next to my dog."

Somehow their confessions lightened the load. It helped Tanda to shake off the stark terror she'd felt when that thing in the sky had careened toward them. "I thought it was going to kill us all. Thought it was the end, and we'd die never knowing what *this* is all about."

"For a moment, I thought I had to be dreaming," Miles admitted. "It was all so surreal."

"Which part?" Logan's smile in the near darkness was like a beacon.

Tanda had no idea how he did it, how he kept a calm perspective as the world was literally falling apart. Before she could analyze it, he started laughing. Miles joined him, and she couldn't help but laugh with them and shake her head at these two men by her side.

They were more than amigos.

Campañeros, perhaps.

Partners.

Maybe the laughter was the aftereffect of so much adrenaline buzzing through her veins. Tanda wanted to set this moment in her memory—not being needed by anyone, knowing that for the moment they had done a good job, sitting with friends and enjoying an evening breeze.

Logan was her friend and had been for many years.

And Miles? She wasn't sure, but she thought he could be. Something had passed between them as the falling object bore down on them, as she'd turned with a child under one arm and a mutt under the other, unsure what she would do or where she'd run.

At that moment her gaze had landed on Miles, and some deep knowledge had sent shivers down her spine. The memory brought with it the terror of their situation and threatened to turn her laughter to sobs.

She cleared her throat, tried again to push the fear back. "Best guess on what the thing was that fell from the sky?"

Logan was sitting across from her, also leaning against one of the gazebo posts, his eyes now closed. "I'll tell you what it wasn't—in my opinion. It wasn't a rocket. At least it didn't seem to have the elongated shape of a rocket. Besides, who would aim a rocket at Alpine? There's nothing here anyone could possibly want to destroy."

"Probably not a plane either," Tanda said. "We haven't seen one of those since last Tuesday. Plus, Grant and Makowski would have seen flames—there would have been fuel burning at the crash site."

That's what Tanda kept telling herself.

It wasn't a plane.

They couldn't have saved anyone, even if they had dashed to the site, if they'd been able to find the site.

"But that sound..." Miles stared up at the sky, as if he could recreate the thing—the sight and sound of it—and figure out exactly what it was. "It was such a high-pitched sound. Something with a lot of altitude and coming in fast. I would guess a meteor or a satellite."

"Huh." Tanda didn't know what to say to that.

"Could have been a meteor," Logan agreed. "But usually the news hype those up weeks before they hit—so everyone can go outside and get a good view. I don't remember any mention of one before the stations went off-line."

"So a satellite?" Tanda was thinking of her brother's screen shots. Of his theory that it had to be either terrorism or a natural event. Which of those would explain a falling satellite? And how would that cause the electricity to go out in Alpine, Texas?

Miles stood and whistled to Zeus, who stretched once then clambered to his feet.

"Your dog looks tired, Doc."

Miles smiled, the first genuine smile she could remember seeing from him.

"We both are."

Logan and Tanda stood as well, and the three of them walked back toward the business section of Alpine. The night was quiet. No riots for the moment. No town residents attacking each other.

Miles peeled off at the medical office, calling out a soft "goodnight" as he went.

Logan's place was over by the college. He stopped in the middle of the intersection where she needed to turn right to her apartment. "We're not responding fast enough to this, not doing the things we need to do."

"Such as?"

"Meeting with the Sul Ross faculty and students."

"Isn't that the mayor's job?"

"I don't know that we can depend on Melinda or Ben to do what needs to be done."

"Agreed, but at the same time..." She hesitated, but then she realized that now probably was the time to voice her concerns. "If I'm seen pushing into areas that aren't under my department, Melinda or Ben could make trouble."

"Maybe an unofficial meeting then."

"Okay."

Tanda thought of Owen, the tweaker she'd held in her jail because he'd been stupid or desperate enough to try and steal a woman's purse. She'd released him earlier that day, reminding him that charges had been filed and he would be held accountable for the attempted burglary once they had a sitting judge.

She cleared her throat and said, "I'm worried about our repeat offender population."

"Users?"

"Yeah." She rubbed the muscle in her neck. "And the vulnerable population—elderly, those who require regular medication, the half a dozen women who are pregnant."

"That's a lot of worry for you to carry around." He looked at her, his expression a mixture of kindness and reproach. "You can't do it all, Chief Lopez."

Her *abuela*'s words whispered through her mind.

You're trying to do everyone's job, and that is several jobs too many.

"Make a list of your concerns. We'll tackle them one by one."

"We?" She tried to make it sound light-hearted, teasing, but it came out more like a frightened kitten's meow.

"Me and you. Maybe that doc you coerced into taking Fielder's place. We'll be the three musketeers and set it all to rights."

"*Tres mosqueteros.*" She laughed. "I like the sound of that."

"Goodnight, Chief."

"Goodnight, Logan."

She walked to her apartment, trying to shake the sense of heaviness and impending doom that had so quickly returned. They were surviving. They were doing all right, and perhaps it wasn't the end of the world. Perhaps the cavalry would come.

She pulled out the pocket notepad and stared at it—a small wire spiral at the top and lined pages that were 3-inch by 4-inch. She sat at her kitchen table, moonlight pooling in through the open window, and began the list of things she needed to do.

Or delegate.

After all, she was only one woman.

Chapter 12

T HE SITUATION WORSENED THROUGH the rest of the week. Her officers were called to the artist district at least once a day to deal with broken windows, harassment, even some thefts. The artists, led by Gonzo, were convinced the ranchers were attempting to run them out of town. Tanda wasn't so sure. Ranchers had their hands full trying to switch to dry-land farming and taking care of their animals. This felt like frustrated people with time on their hands.

Teenagers?

Tweakers?

Whoever the guilty persons were, she hadn't caught them yet, but she would.

On top of the problem in the arts district, Mayor Stone was on a roll, coming unraveled before their eyes. Saturday's required meeting ended with Melinda screaming at Emmanuel Garcia to find her more supplies, though how he was supposed to do that was anyone's guess.

Dixie and Ron were waiting for Tanda when she exited the building.

"You need to talk to her." Dixie fell into step on her right, Ron on her left.

"Melinda? She's not going to listen to me. From what we just saw in there, she's not going to listen to anyone."

"But we have to try." Dixie's voice was tight, frustrated.

Ron put a hand on Tanda's arm to stop her. "Someone's been in the supply barns and taken out several pallets of food."

He shook his head, anticipating her question. "I don't know how it could have happened. That barn is locked up tight, and I've had workers from my department standing guard in shifts."

"They didn't see anything?"

"No. Except..." He pulled in a breath, glanced around as if to assure himself they couldn't be overheard. "Melinda stopped by there yesterday. She demanded my people go to city hall and fill out some hazardous duty forms. Of course when they arrived at city hall, no one knew what she was talking about."

Tanda put her hands on her hips, just above her gun belt and stared up at the sky for a moment. Finally, she sighed. "I still don't know what I can do."

"Talk to Ben," Dixie suggested.

"He might listen to you." Ron didn't look away. Instead, he held her gaze, waiting until she'd nodded that she would try.

So she'd turned around and walked back into the building, even though she now had eight pages of items written in her little notebook that all needed to be done yesterday. She found Ben staring at the vending machine in the employees' lunch room. Someone had removed the glass. The only thing left in the machine was a pack of gum.

"Don't arrest me for stealing, Chief." He reached into the machine, grabbed the gum, stripped away the end of the wrapping and offered her one.

She shook her head, then said, "We need to talk."

Ben stared at the empty machine. "Not here."

They walked out the front door of the building into June sunshine splashing over the concrete. The day was still warm, though it was nearly six in the evening.

Tanda stopped and waited for Ben to turn and face her. He was officially the mayor pro tem. His job was to support the mayor, understand the mayor's duties, and stand in for the mayor when necessary. She'd known Ben for a very long time. It was sometimes difficult to conceive that he was the same classmate she'd gone to school with for twelve years. What had happened to him? And were the changes irreversible? She thought of Dixie and Ron, of the worry on their faces, of the supplies that the town needed.

"Melinda's out of control."

Ben shrugged, but he still didn't look at her. Instead he walked over to where city hall's decorative fountain should be bubbling. The concrete bottom was lined with blue tiles, as was the knee-high rim. Both sparkled in the sun, winked at her as if to say, "Did you expect life to always be shimmering pools of water?"

No water flowed there now. Instead there was a stagnant pool of water, coins glittering from the bottom.

Tanda sat on the rim.

"She stole supplies, Ben. Those supplies are for the town."

"She's the mayor, something you seem to forget." Now he turned on her, his face hard like the concrete of the pool, his expression a sneer. "Those supplies are to be used at her discretion."

"This isn't going to work. She can't go on like this."

"If you don't like the job she's doing, start the process for a recall."

Tanda stared at him in disbelief. The process to recall an elected official was time-consuming and laborious. The last time it had been tried was in 2013—albeit unsuccessfully.

She stood with her arms crossed, feet firmly planted, ready to battle her childhood friend if it was necessary. "You are insane if you think the people of Alpine are going to stand by and allow their mayor to pilfer supplies while I file an affidavit for recall, gather signatures, and then hold a special election. What world are you living in, Ben?"

"The same world as before the train crash, Tanda. Aren't you the one who is all for upholding law and order?"

"Law and order is one thing." She was angry now, shaking with adrenaline and outrage. "Politics is another. We cannot afford to embrace business as usual. I had three more people die today, Ben. Three more people. One was our geography teacher. Not only did I not have the means to save them, I didn't even know they were dead until the neighbors notified us of the smell."

She saw a crack in his demeanor—small, nearly imperceptible, fleeting. Still, she pounced on it. "You know this is not right, and you know it won't end well. You need to get on the correct side of things before that happens."

"Sounds like a threat, Tanda."

"Sounds like sound advice, Ben."

She stormed away, her left eye twitching and her pulse racing. It took a good twenty minutes before she had enough control of her emotions to check in at the office. Edna was working extra hours. They all were, and it couldn't continue indefinitely.

"Nothing new, Chief. Maybe you should get some rest."

Instead Tanda walked into her office, shut the door, and tried to get a grip of the situation. But there was no gripping a collapse of this magnitude. Why hadn't they heard from anyone outside of Alpine? What was happening in the rest of the state...in the rest of the country? How would they survive if they received no additional supplies?

She went home and fell into a dreamless sleep for a mere four hours, then she was awake, going over her lists, determined to do whatever she could to see her town through this disaster. She would not let people like Melinda Stone and Ben Cason win. She would not give in to the Gonzos of the world.

Saturday was no better, with a small fire on the west side of town and a car-jacking near the university. That afternoon she spent like every other day, trying to maintain a hold on a situation that was quickly unraveling.

Sunday morning brought rain—much needed rain. The smell of it soothed her soul. That scent seemed clean somehow, and she had the thought that if the rain could heal the dry parched land, maybe it could also bring forth hope.

She worked through the morning, then rode out to her parents for lunch and was surprised to find Keme and Lucy there. Years ago they'd met every Sunday for lunch, when Keme's children were young, when her parents weren't yet gray, when her *abuela* could stand straight and strong.

The visit should have eased the knots in her shoulders, but she couldn't even force herself to eat. How long would their food last? How would they get more insulin for *Abuela*? What should they be doing now to prepare for winter?

Before she left, Keme took her aside and told her he'd repaired their pop's old CB radio.

"And does it work?"

"So far...mostly static. My guess is that it has a range of thirty miles. I did catch a guy from Fort Davis. He was saying something about a perimeter around the town, but then either his radio went dead or he was interrupted."

"Okay."

What did that mean? A perimeter around Fort Davis? To keep people in or to keep people out?

"Be careful, Sis."

"Of course."

She rode Roxy back into town, thinking about Fort Davis, wondering what was happening there. She had never felt so isolated, and somehow being isolated made her feel vulnerable. How could she protect the citizens of Alpine against things they couldn't see? How could she protect them against their own mayor?

Roxy noticed the activity downtown before she did, pricking her ears forward and picking up her pace. Was that music she was hearing? And definitely the smell of grilled meat. And people, lots of people. There wasn't any shouting. No shots fired. It was more like the sounds and smells of the farmer's market or concessions for a baseball game at Kokernot field.

She pressed her heels lightly to Roxy's side and the mare needed no additional encouragement. They trotted into downtown.

Chapter 13

MILES LOOKED UP AS Tanda led her horse through the crowd. He whistled to get her attention, then waved her over to their table.

Logan stood and reached for her horse's lead rope. "I'll take care of Roxy. Don't eat all the food before I get back."

Tanda sank into a chair next to Miles. She continued to look around, as if she were trying to reconcile the events of the past few days with what she was seeing.

Barbecue grills lined one side of the street.

Children played on the town green.

People laughed and smiled and sat in front of heaping plates of food.

"You have a good town here and good people."

She finally looked over at Miles, then cocked her head. "Isn't it Sunday night, or did I misplace a day somewhere? You shouldn't be here until tomorrow."

A week ago, he would have been offended. That seemed like a different life than the one he was living now. He felt changed in some fundamental way, though he couldn't have explained how.

"Yeah, well. Alpine has a way of growing on a person."

"Says the doctor hiding in a cabin."

Miles laughed.

"Might have worked too, if you hadn't found me." He reached down and patted Zeus. "We decided to walk down tonight so I could get an early start tomorrow. I was...uh...worried about some of my patients."

She arched an eyebrow, but she didn't push.

When Logan returned they grabbed a paper plate—something Miles suspected would soon be a thing of the past—and started at the far end of the line of grills, Zeus trotting at his side.

Pork chops and steaks and sizzling chicken.

Hamburgers and hotdogs—though there were no buns.

But there was lettuce from people's gardens, along with fresh tomatoes, canned pickles, and grilled corn. At the end of the row someone had placed large jugs of water and red solo cups. Next to that was a giant cooler filled with warm soft drinks, with a handwritten sign that read *please take only one*.

It was an end-of-days celebration.

And Miles understood that the town needed it. They needed to celebrate what had been and set in their minds this image of better days. Of abundance. They needed to believe that it was something they would have again. The two biggest questions were how long until that day, and what hardships they would encounter in the meantime.

They sat back down at the card table Miles had brought from his medical office. *His* medical office? He supposed it was. He broke a hot dog into pieces and set it on the extra plate he'd snagged for Zeus. Tanda laughed and added the skin from her chicken. Logan broke off half a hamburger patty.

"You two are going to make my dog fat."

But he appreciated the kindness, as did Zeus.

"As a physician, I can't condone this sort of eating." He waved a fork filled with hamburger and a piece of lettuce. "Bad for the arteries."

"That piece of lettuce will save you, Doc." Tanda's plate was full, like his and Logan's.

Miles realized he couldn't remember seeing her eat before.

They focused on the food and on enjoying the evening, but no one went back for seconds. They were full. Sated.

Someone brought out a guitar. Another person began to tap a rhythm on a bongo drum. The music faded into the background, and it seemed to Miles that he was listening to a symphony of sorts—the voices momentarily free from worry, the children laughing, the grills still sizzling as more meat was cooked.

And then an older couple stood and walked to an area that had been cleared of tables and chairs. The man was thin and once tall, though bent now. It was impossible to tell whether his dark skin was from his heritage or hours in the sun. He wore jeans, a faded western shirt, and an old cowboy hat. She was rounder, at least a foot shorter, and wore a traditional Mexican skirt. She walked into his arms and they began to dance to the music as they must have done a hundred times before.

Miles felt tears prick his eyes. Why now? Why this? A couple, enjoying a moment of tenderness. But more than all he'd seen, that single image reminded him of all he'd lost.

Tanda saved him from falling back into the well of pity that had become his second home. She pushed her plate away, folded her arms on the table, and declared, "I need to know what's going on."

Miles thought she was kidding. He almost said, "Don't we all," but then he noticed her expression. *Grave* was the word that came to mind.

Logan, too, pushed his plate away, and focused completely on her.

"I can't...we can't...know how to prepare people if we don't know what's happened." She looked up at them. "We're smart—the town doctor, area vet, and local police chief. We should be able to figure this out."

Logan stood, gathered up their plates, and dumped them in a nearby trash can. Returning, he crossed his legs and flicked his gaze from Tanda to Miles and back again. "I'm game. Let's do this."

Miles looked back toward the drink table. "Hang on..." he strode over to it, spoke with Elizabeth Lujan, little Bethany's mom. "How's my patient?"

"She's very good, doctor. Thank you for asking."

"Bring her in tomorrow and let me check how that arm is healing."

"I will."

He nodded toward the pad of paper and pen that she'd used to write *please take only one.* "May I borrow that?"

"Of course. Keep it."

But he realized that even a pad of paper was now a precious commodity. "I'll give it back to you tomorrow." He smiled his thanks and hurried back to Logan and Tanda.

"Okay, let's list any possibility. Give me your craziest idea. Anything goes. Ready?" Whatever they called out, he chronicled down the left side of the page.

Earthquakes

Solar flares

Global warming

Russians

Chinese

Domestic terrorists

Meteors

Asteroids

Aliens

Zombies

Volcanoes

Nuclear attack

Artificial Intelligence revolt

Finally, he capped the pen, dropped it on the pad, and sat back. "Looks like we've listed the plot for every apocalyptic movie made in the last twenty-five years."

"Feels rather good to see them written down, though." Tanda spun the pad toward her and picked up the pen.

"If you know the enemy and know yourself, you need not fear the results of a hundred battles." Logan smiled sheepishly when they stared at him. "Sun Tzu, Chinese philosopher."

"Strange thing for a vet to know, but okay." Mile's smile stretched across his face. The enormous amount of protein he'd just digested must be affecting his mood. Perhaps it was simply putting down the burden of his patients if only for a single meal. He felt...*buoyant*.

"Now let's look at this logically." Tanda uncapped the pen and began to cross things out. "Earthquakes wouldn't take out all communication. Can't be a solar flare—cars are working. Global warming wouldn't be so sudden." Looking up, she asked, "What's the difference between a meteor and an asteroid?"

"A meteor is a small piece of an asteroid." Logan's voice was now serious.

Tanda put a question mark beside those two. Then she crossed out aliens and zombies.

Miles took the pen from her, and though he was looking upside down, he crossed out volcanoes, nuclear attack, and AI revolt.

"You sure?"

"Reasonably so."

"Okay."

She put a star beside the lines that read *Russians, Chinese, domestic terrorists*. "This answers who, not what." Then she told them about her brother Keme and the screenshots he'd taken before the train crash.

"So an airplane suffered an uncontrolled descent, and that was followed by satellite news going off-line, then the stock market falling."

"Right. All before our two trains crashed into one another." Tanda shook her head. "But what could those things possibly have to do with one another?"

"The internet..." Miles cleared his throat, suddenly wishing for more water. "All those things run, to one degree or another, off 4G."

"And 4G is dependent on satellite technology. It's not just that the internet is out. It could be..." Logan shook his head, then finally met their gaze. "It could be the entire satellite array has gone off-line. That would affect airline travel, communication, shipping and receiving, trains..."

Tanda pressed her fingertips to a spot above her left eye. Her voice dropped to a mere whisper. "Not just off line, but falling from the sky."

"Maybe." Miles tried to put more conviction behind the word. "Maybe, but it's still just...just a theory."

It was their best theory. The only thing left on their sheet of paper was the list of culprits and the words *meteors* and *asteroids*. He knew that one large meteor could do significant damage. Hell, current scientific theory held that a large meteor had killed the dinosaurs and brought on the last ice age.

They were still here though, dancing in the street, filling their bellies with food that tomorrow or the next day would have gone bad. It didn't seem likely that even an array of meteors could cause the outages they were seeing without also causing physical damage around them.

He glanced to his left and right, as if to assure himself that the businesses along Fifth Street remained intact. Then he turned the paper toward him, uncapped the pen and wrote *satellite malfunctions.*

"I have to go to Fort Davis." Tanda popped to her feet, then sat back down. "The people who work at the McDonald Observatory—they'll know. They'll know what we're dealing with, and once we know, then..."

"We'll know how to prepare." Logan nodded in agreement, already on board with the idea, practically packing his bags.

"How do we know we can even get there? You said...you said that no one who's left town has come back."

"We will. We will get there, and we will come back. Keme told me he heard there's a perimeter around Fort Davis, but we'll get past that, get to the observatory, and find some answers." Tanda turned all her attention on Miles, and he again felt that zap. He told himself it wasn't sexual. It wasn't merely the force of her personality or the desperation in her eyes.

It was fate.

Destiny.

That which is predetermined and sure to come true.

He didn't know the what or who of their current situation. He certainly didn't know how they would travel to another town and safely return. But he did know that the three of them—yes, Logan was somehow destined to be in the mix as well—the three of them were here, at this point in time, at this place in nowhere Texas for a reason.

He wasn't a deeply spiritual man. The last threads of the faith he'd been raised in had dropped away when his wife and daughter were killed. What he was experiencing at that moment wasn't a spiritual feeling, not in the traditional sense.

It was more of a knowing.

And that knowing easily trumped his scientific training, because there had been things that he'd seen that couldn't be easily explained. He was a man of science, but a year alone in a remote cabin had taught him that there was more to life than he would ever understand.

He would go to Fort Davis if for no other reason than to face his destiny.

Chapter 14

T HEY DIDN'T LEAVE THE next day. Miles had patients to see. Logan was now making visits to area farms to check if anyone had animals that needed attention. Tanda needed to ask Rodriguez to take her shift on Tuesday.

"I don't mind taking your shift, Chief. And we both know the promise of overtime means little. There's no one to issue a paycheck. Even if there were, there's nothing to buy with the money."

"Yeah. I'm aware." It had bothered her that she was asking her officers to work for free, or nearly that. "When our digital infrastructure comes back on line, and for now I'm going to believe it will one day, then I'll make sure you're paid every penny you're owed."

"That's not what I'm worried about." Jorge sat forward in the chair across from her desk, elbows on his knees, hands clasped together. "Do you think going is smart, Chief? We don't know what's happening out there, but I can tell you it isn't good."

Tanda thought of the small spiral notepad she now carried in her shirt pocket. Every day she added more pages of tasks, of worries, of uncertainties. She didn't even know where to begin on those lists, because she didn't understand what had happened.

"I'm not going alone. Logan and Doc Turner will be with me."

"We have one doctor and one vet. If they don't come back...if you don't come back—"

"We'll come back, but staying here, not knowing—that isn't a valid option."

"They're both bad choices."

"Yeah. I get that."

He stood slowly, and Tanda noticed for the first time the dark circles under his eyes, the weariness in his shoulders. She wasn't the only one carrying an extra load of responsibility. "How's Yvonne?"

"She's okay. Worried that she can't contact her parents in San Angelo, but she's okay."

"And the kids?"

"The three youngest think it's any other summer day." He glanced out the window, stared off into the distance as if he could see what was coming, then shook his head. "My two older ones though, they understand that their life has changed."

"Thank you for doing this."

"Thank me by coming home."

She met with Ron Mullins, Dixie Peters, and Emmanuel Garcia that afternoon. There was nothing in the city's bylaws that said they couldn't meet, but they were all quite aware of what the mayor's reaction would be should she find out.

"So you're going because you're looking for answers." Emmanuel shook his head. "I don't know, Tanda. Sounds dangerous."

"Think of it this way. We have a storehouse of emergency supplies, but we don't know how long this situation is going to last. We don't know if those supplies need to be enough for the summer or for the next year."

Ron Mullins ran a hand up and over the top of his bald head. Finally, he sighed and said, "I agree it needs to be done, and I'm glad that Logan and Dr. Turner are both going with you. But this town needs the three of you—"

Tanda held up a hand. "Already heard that lecture from Jorge. We'll come back. I promise you that."

"You can only promise that you'll try," Dixie pointed out.

Later that evening, as Tanda was heating up a can of soup on a camping stove she'd rigged in the kitchen, with the adjacent window propped open—actually all the windows in her apartment were open—she heard a knock on the door.

Dixie stood in the breezeway, dressed in jeans and an old Kokernot Field t-shirt, and holding what looked like a gym bag. "I come bearing gifts."

Seeing the steam rising from the pot on the camping stove, she said, "Eat first. While it's hot."

"There's enough to share."

"I won't turn it down."

They ate hearty beef stew with crackers and the last of Tanda's cheese. When they'd both rinsed their dishes, Dixie unzipped the bag and began pulling out items. "Three bio-hazard masks."

"For?"

"No idea. Just seemed like you should have them." Next she pulled out an axe, a first aid kit, and an emergency radio. "We haven't been able to reach anyone on this yet, but maybe when you're at the observatory you can."

The last thing she pulled out was a handheld device with a small screen and several buttons. She pushed the blue button in the middle, and the screen lit up with a blue background and two sets of numbers—all zero.

"This will alert you to dangerous levels of radiation. If the screen turns red and this indicator starts flashing, back away from whatever you're close to."

Tanda thought of the object that had nearly crashed into their first city-wide meeting. Had it been radioactive? She hadn't even considered such a thing.

"Thanks, Dixie. Seriously. I appreciate it. I never would have thought of these things, though..." She reached for the axe, picked it up, and grinned. "Not really sure what scenario would require this."

"Better to have it and not need it..."

"Than need it and not have it. Yeah. Agreed."

Dixie was single, like Tanda. She lived with a boyfriend who was a firemen in Fort Stockton. His schedule was twenty-four hours on, forty-eight hours off. He'd been at work when whatever happened occurred.

"I imagine you're worried about Hunter, but he's a smart guy. He'll find a way to make it home."

Dixie didn't speak for a moment. She glanced around the room, out the window, down at the table top. Finally she met Tanda's gaze. "I know he's smart and resourceful, but if he were going to make it home, I think he'd already be here."

"Don't write him off. You keep believing."

"And now you sound like my mom."

"She's a wise woman."

Dixie put the items back into the gym bag and zipped it closed. "Hunter and I had just decided to have a family, that it was time. And now this—"

"This is a giant question mark in our path, but it isn't the end."

Dixie shrugged. It was plain that she was preoccupied about something. Something more serious than a missing loved one?

Tanda braced herself and asked, "What is it?"

"I attended disaster training when I first came here, and I keep thinking about something they said. They called it *The 3 Principles For Whole Community.*"

"Sounds enticing."

Dixie held up a finger, "Number one. Understand and meet the needs of your community. That's why I'm not trying to stop you, Tanda. We don't understand what the needs are yet, so we have no chance of meeting them."

"Agreed." She walked Dixie to the door, stepped outside with her, stared up at the stars that had become increasingly brighter over the last two weeks with no pollution to mar the heavenly view. "What were the other two principles?"

"Engage and empower all parts of the community."

"We certainly aren't doing that."

"And strengthen what works well." Dixie crossed her arms and leveled her gaze on Tanda. "We have to do step one first. Good luck tomorrow."

Tanda thought she'd stay awake that night, tossing and turning and worrying. She didn't. Though the room was still warm and there was no fan to offer relief, she didn't lie awake. She fell asleep as soon as her head settled on the pillow, and it was a good sleep, perhaps the first one she'd had since the collapse. She rose ten minutes before her alarm went off feeling better than she had in days. Maybe it was the fact that they were doing something, that they were going on the offense rather than simply reacting to things they didn't understand.

She didn't wear her uniform. Instead she pulled on her freshest pair of jeans and a clean white t-shirt. She stuck her ID, including her badge, into her back packet. She slid her handgun into a hip holster, then donned a short-sleeved cotton blouse that she left unbuttoned over the t-shirt. Pulling on a Sul Ross ball cap, she pulled the strap of her backpack over her right shoulder and hefted Dixie's duffle with her left.

She was approaching the doctor's office when Miles stepped outside and nodded at her, Zeus at his side. They both turned at the sound of Logan's Jeep. They'd spent twenty minutes on Sunday evening deciding whether to drive or take the horses. In the end, they decided if there ever was a task that needed to be done quickly, this one did.

Plus, she still couldn't quite fathom what had happened to the people they'd sent out of town. Had someone stopped them? Hurt them? If so, if it was other people they were up against, they'd have a better chance of outrunning trouble in a Jeep than on a horse. At least, that's what she told herself.

Miles and Zeus took the back seats.

The duffel from Dixie went on the floorboard between them.

Tanda sat up front, next to Logan, her own backpack at her feet where she could reach it quickly. It held another gun, extra ammunition, water, food, and her personal first aid kit. She noticed that Miles had his medical bag.

They drove north on Texas Highway 118 which took them past Kokernot Field, the Regional Medical Center that had no doctors but was still attempting to care for a few patients, and the municipal airport.

The airport looked abandoned.

Tanda pulled out her notebook, added *speak to airport director* to her list, and returned it to her pocket.

They had the road to themselves.

Tanda wanted to enjoy the morning. The sun spilled across the landscape, and the air was cooler now. She wanted to appreciate this moment of respite, but she couldn't. Too much adrenaline coursed through her veins, and it felt as if her subconscious was knock, knock, knocking on her brain. She repeatedly clenched then flexed her hands. Logan glanced her way, then returned his attention to the road. They were going well under the speed limit, intent on seeing anything unusual—anything that didn't belong.

They were twenty miles north of town when they spied the crater. They'd driven out of the mountains that separated Alpine from Fort Davis, and the land had leveled out. The view was uninterrupted for miles—except for the thing that had crashed into the desert.

Logan slowed. "Do we stop, or keep going?"

"We're here for answers," Tanda said.

Miles nodded in agreement. "That might just hold some."

They parked the Jeep. Zeus was the first one out, relieving himself on some scrub brush. Walking three abreast, they approached the thing that had fallen from the sky, but they stopped well back from the crater.

"This has to be what we heard last Wednesday night." Miles was wearing sunglasses and a ball cap. He carried his medical bag in his left hand, but it was plain from the destruction around them that there was no one to save.

The object was roughly the size of a Volkswagen bus.

Logan used his phone to snap a few pictures.

Tanda unzipped Dixie's bag and pulled out the radiation detector. She pushed the blue button in the middle, and the screen lit up with a blue background and two sets of numbers. They weren't zero, but neither was the red alert button flashing.

"I guess there is radiation, but at low levels. Dixie said if the screen turns red—"

"Back carefully away." Miles shrugged when they both turned to stare at him. "Docs do disaster training too."

They walked closer to the crater. Tanda thought it looked like twisted metal though she couldn't put a name to any of the pieces she was seeing. The numbers on the device she was holding began to climb, and then, when they were still a good thirty feet away, the background on the screen turned red. She stopped, frozen in place.

"It's okay. We don't need to go any closer." Logan pulled down his ballcap. "We've seen all we need to here."

Miles called to Zeus, and they returned to the Jeep.

"So we know it's radioactive..." What else did they know? Tanda's mind went blank.

"It didn't look like a missile," Logan said, pulling back onto the road. "Not that I've seen one up close, but if you asked me, it didn't look like a warhead of any sort."

"Satellite," Miles offered.

"Yup."

They continued on, trying to make sense of what they'd seen, trying to come up with at least a theory of what had happened. Tanda felt as if she were trying to put a jigsaw together by studying the blank back side. Nothing made sense.

The road remained empty. Occasionally they could see a farmhouse in the distance and once they saw a man plowing a field with a horse. Two weeks out from the event, and they were living like pioneers.

Logan cleared his throat. "Looks like Keme was right about the perimeter."

They were still two miles southeast of Fort Davis, but they slowed and then stopped well back of the makeshift roadblock. A variety of pick-up trucks, semis, and heavy equipment had been placed across the road. They were positioned so that a person could drive through, but slowly, maneuvering around the vehicles. And they stretched a good quarter mile away from the road in both directions.

Before they could decide whether to attempt to drive through, two men stepped out from the lead vehicle.

Both were carrying rifles.

The one on the left lifted a hand indicating they should stop. When he saw Tanda step out of the Jeep, he motioned to the other guy that everything was okay and then walked toward them.

"Tanda..." He slipped the rifle to his left hand so that he could shake with her and Logan, then moved the rifle back to his right.

His ease with the rifle appeared too natural for Tanda's comfort. He looked as if he'd been doing this all his life, but he hadn't. Roger Wakeland was a local mechanic. Tanda had used him twice when she'd had problems with their police cruisers. Apparently, he'd closed shop since there were few if any vehicles to work on. And what...taken up the job of city guard?

"What's going on, Roger?"

He shrugged. "We put the perimeter up a week ago."

"Why?"

"To protect what's ours." His welcoming smile had turned to a frown.

"From whom?" Miles asked.

"Whoever wants it, that's who." He again shifted the rifle and turned his gaze to Logan. "You know what it's like out here.

Ranchers aren't going to sit around and wait for the feds to show up and make everything okay."

"Are you worried about people coming down from I-10?" Logan asked.

"That has happened, a couple of times. Some of them are okay folks, but we sent them on their way."

"What does that mean?" Tanda crossed her arms. "You're saying you wouldn't let them stay here?"

"I'm saying that we need to keep what we have for the people who belong here."

"Any other problems?" Miles asked. "Any other people or groups that we should be aware of?"

Roger didn't answer Miles. In fact, he was looking at him as if he didn't belong there, as if he was going to tell Miles to get back in the Jeep and head the other way.

"This is Miles Turner," Tanda explained. "Our doctors were all caught out of town when this thing started—all except Doc Fielder who died from a heart attack the first week. Miles has stepped up to fill in that gap."

Roger shrugged, but he didn't offer to shake hands.

"We're only passing through," Miles added. "If there's anything that we need to know, anyone we need to be on the lookout for…"

"Yes, there is." Roger swiped at the sweat on his forehead. "I've heard of three different bands of folks. I've only seen them from a distance, myself, but the stories…they're enough to keep you awake at night."

Tanda had reached the end of her patience. "Meaning what, exactly?"

"Meaning that they'll kill you for the gas in your tank."

"Any theories as to what has happened...what caused everything to stop working?"

"Yeah, plenty of theories. Everything from radicals taking over the government to aliens."

"Okay." Tanda shook her head, tried to shake off the tension that was building in her neck. "We need through."

"I'll have to call for an escort."

"Tell me you're kidding."

"Look, Tanda..." He stepped closer and lowered his voice. "In general, we're not letting people through. Most folks have to turn back or take one of the unpaved county roads around. But you being the police chief and all, I'm pretty sure that Jim will make an exception."

"Jim Bennett?"

"Yeah."

"Are you telling me he's in charge?"

"He is, and he's the reason people are safe in their homes at night."

"What happened to your mayor and your police chief?"

"Chief Sanderson stepped aside, said he was too old to be dealing with the apocalypse."

"And Simon Banks?"

"Killed, in his sleep."

Tanda thought she must have heard him wrong. She shook her head, realized he was serious, and tried to wrap her mind around what he'd said.

"It happened last week. One of those groups I told you about hit us in the middle of the night. Killed nine people, took cars, ammunition, food supplies...and they did it quietly. They even rolled the cars out so we wouldn't hear the motors. But a few people tried to intercede. They were the ones killed. Most of us didn't know what was happening until the screaming started. Simon's wife...she still hasn't come to terms with it."

"That was when you put up the perimeter." Logan addressed Roger, but his gaze constantly scanned the horizon.

"Yeah."

"We'd appreciate the escort, Roger. Thank you."

Miles nodded to the north. "Has anyone been up to the observatory?"

"Nah. We have enough to deal with down here."

Thirty minutes later they were headed north out of town.

"I can't believe it," Tanda admitted. "It's only been two weeks and they're acting like this is the Wild West."

Miles had his hand on top of Zeus's head, settling the dog who seemed on high alert. "Folks do what they have to do in order to feel safe."

"Ransack another town? Indiscriminately kill people? And for what? A few gallons of gas?"

"We're here to find out what happened and to see where things stand." Logan jerked his thumb back toward Fort Davis. "That tells us where things stand, at least for the people in Fort Davis. I would bet if they're responding with drastic measures, other towns are doing the same."

"Why haven't these thugs hit Alpine?" Miles asked.

"Fort Davis is closer to I-10."

"Fort Stockton is closer to Alpine," Tanda murmured.

"True, but picture it on the map. If they're coming from Fort Stockton, which seems likely, two-thirds of the trip to Fort Davis is via I-10."

"Why would they prefer a major freeway?" Miles stared out the window to the east.

"More people to prey upon, maybe."

Tanda didn't think things were adding up. The sooner they made it to the observatory, the sooner they made it home, the better.

She'd actually convinced herself that it would be nice to be out of the confines of Alpine, to be freed of her responsibilities there, if only for a few hours. Now, all she could think of was that she hadn't given enough consideration to what they might find.

Chapter 15

"WHAT DO YOU MEAN, they're gone?" Melinda felt her blood pressure rising. She needed a bath, a martini, and a massage...though she wasn't sure that was the order she'd prefer. "When?"

"They left early this morning."

"They?"

"Tanda, Doc Turner, and Logan Wright."

"Where were they going?"

"No one knows."

"Meaning you don't know."

"Meaning no one knows. Trust me. They didn't tell anyone."

Melinda tapped her fingernails against the marble top of her desk. She needed a manicure. She needed out of this two-bit town. Perhaps staying here had been a mistake.

Her gaze drifted to the framed *Texas Monthly* article on the wall. *Alpine Texas—A Well Cultivated Oasis.* The photograph of her was especially good. It had been taken back when there were still manicurists and hair stylists. What were these people doing if not working? Not that she'd ever used anyone local. She preferred the salons in San Antonio. Everyone knows that service people gossip, and she did not need that sort of attention from her constituents.

"Find out where they went. Find out why they went there, and in the meantime we'll..."

No, she wasn't quite ready to share that information yet. She would, when and if she needed to. She flicked her gaze up. "Go and get me some information. Find out what they're doing, what they're planning. If you can't do as simple a task as that, don't bother coming back at all."

Chapter 16

"TELL ME ABOUT THE observatory." Miles leaned forward, his head between the two front seats so that he could hear their reply.

"It's technically a part of The University of Texas system. Originally built and funded by William Johnson McDonald from Paris, Texas." Logan rubbed a hand across the back of his neck. "He was a banker who left the bulk of his fortune to UT to endow an astronomical observatory."

"Do they have a staff?"

"Yes," Tanda answered. "At least they did last time I was here. Tour guides, that sort of thing. It's been years, though, since I've visited the place. You know how it is. When something is close to where you live it tends to fade into the background. But people come from all over to look through the big telescopes and see the night sky."

"And scientists apply years in advance for telescope time." Logan shrugged. "The last time I toured the observatory, they explained that a lot of that work is now done remotely. A technician adjusts the position of the telescope and the scientist requesting the data is able to watch it through a live feed from home."

"Not anymore they aren't." Tanda shifted in her seat to smile back at Miles. "I'll bet you didn't realize we had an amateur astronomer in our midst, but Logan is a real star gazer."

Logan laughed. "My parents gave me a telescope for my twelfth birthday."

"You still have it."

"I do. Back in sixth grade, I was sure I was going to be the first to identify life on another planet. Or maybe see its spaceship pass by." His voice lightened at the memory. "The last time I visited the observatory was probably a year ago...no two years ago. My nieces were visiting from Dallas. One had decided she wanted to be an astrophysicist."

"She might have to rethink that career choice now." Tanda turned again to look at Miles. "It's seventeen miles from Fort Davis, and includes facilities atop Mount Locke and Mount Fowlkes."

Miles had done a little research on Alpine before moving there. He knew that the town sat on a high plateau in the Chihuahua Desert. If he remembered correctly—oh, how he missed being able to Google such things on his phone—the town sat at an elevation of 4500 feet.

The drive was beautiful. Tall, prehistoric rock outcroppings rose above fields that stretched nearly to the horizon. In any other scenario, Logan would consider it peaceful. Today it felt desolate. The final section of the road gained elevation quickly, and suddenly they were in the parking lot of the Frank N. Bash Visitors Center.

It didn't look as if anyone was around—no cars and no one that they could see inside the building, though they did walk around and peek into a few windows. Historical displays documented the building of the observatory. There were hands-on exhibits for the kids, and a gift shop of course.

All quiet.

All empty.

Miles whistled to Zeus, who had wandered toward an adjacent field. They returned to the Jeep, and drove on up to the actual observatory. No one had set up a perimeter of any sort. The scientists—if they were still there—apparently weren't worried about what might come up the mountain.

Logan idled the car at a blue sign with white lettering.

SUMMIT OF MOUNT LOCKE

HIGHEST POINT ON TEXAS HIGHWAYS

THIS ELEVATION 6791

ELEV VALLEY BELOW 5280

TXDOT

It occurred to Miles that he didn't need Google after all.

The valley stretched in front of them like a blanket rolled out across the ground. In the distance, he thought he could make out the Chisos Mountains, or that might have been his imagination. Red-roofed homes could be seen just below the observatory.

"Should we check down there?" he asked.

Tanda shook her head. "Let's try the observatory first."

Logan pulled the Jeep across an empty row of parking spaces. It didn't escape Miles' notice that he left the vehicle pointed toward the road. Was he worried about having to make a quick exit?

They stepped out, stretched, then moved cautiously toward the observatory. Miles called to Zeus as the dog sniffed around a Mountain Laurel.

"What do we do now? Knock?"

But it didn't come to that. In fact, at first it seemed as if they'd made the journey for nothing. They walked around the white-domed building, trying doors that were locked and attempting to look through windows. All of the lights were out.

"Doesn't seem like anyone's home," he murmured.

Tanda walked to the main door and pivoted toward a camera that Miles hadn't even noticed. It was mounted high up on the wall. She pulled out her badge, held it toward the camera, and waited.

Nothing happened.

"Maybe no one's here," Logan offered. "We haven't seen any vehicles."

"Or maybe they want us to think that no one is here." Tanda stuffed her ID wallet back into her pocket, but she didn't move. She stood there, arms crossed, and waited.

"We could try the other observatory buildings." Logan glanced at Miles who nodded.

But he also checked his watch. The day was getting away from them. They'd stopped at the crashed satellite, driven slowly, had to wait for an escort in Fort Davis, and now this. They still had quite a bit of daylight, but he didn't relish squandering it. Something told him that they did not want to be on the road at night.

He and Logan had begun moving back toward the Jeep, Zeus on their heels, when he heard Tanda's sharp intake of breath.

He turned in time to see a young woman wearing a McDonald Observatory tee push open the front door. She glanced left and right, as if assuring herself that no one else was with them, then motioned them inside.

Once they were in, she turned and gave a thumbs-up to another camera positioned high up on the wall inside the room. Whoever was watching must have pushed a remote locking feature, as there was a thud in the door behind them.

So now they were locked inside. That thought was a bit disturbing.

"This way," the young woman said.

Tanda threw a glance at Logan and Miles, then shrugged and followed the woman. She took them up a flight of stairs, then down a long hall and into an office. She didn't follow them in though. Instead, she slipped back into the hall as if she had somewhere important to be. Sitting behind a desk was a black woman in her fifties with short hair that was beginning to gray. She stood as they walked into the room and introduced herself.

"I'm Shanna Scott, Director of the observatory."

"Tanda Lopez, police chief of Alpine."

"Yes, we've met."

Tanda cocked her head, then shrugged. "I'm sorry. I don't remember."

"It was at a festival in Alpine. As I recall, you were called away to break up a scuffle between some teens."

"Those were the days." Tanda smiled, then introduced Miles and Logan.

Scott gestured toward the chairs. When they'd settled into them, Zeus on the floor beside Miles, she asked, "How can I help you?"

"We want to know what happened, and we thought..." Tanda glanced around the office, met Logan's then Miles' gaze. But it was as if the questions were stuck in her throat. She stared at her hands then out the window, blinking back her uncertainty.

Miles thought Shanna Scott was someone who had learned to hold her cards close to her chest. She might answer their questions, but she probably wouldn't volunteer anything—at least not until she was sure they posed no threat. He understood the need to do that because his mind had also begun dividing people into two categories—friends or foes. "We thought you might have the inside scoop on what happened. We came up with a list that included everything from Russians to aliens."

Scott smiled at that, but she still didn't offer anything.

"Everything seems to point to a significant satellite outage," Logan added. He told her about the train crash two weeks earlier. "This morning we passed a crater a few miles north of Alpine. In the middle of the crater was an...an object about the size of a small school bus."

"Did it have anything that looked like solar panels?"

Logan pulled out his phone, tapped and scrolled until he found the photo of the crater, then held it out to Scott.

"That would be a lower orbital satellite. I'm surprised more of it didn't burn up on re-entry, but then we don't know a lot about these things."

Tanda found her voice. "So that's it? That's what's happened? The satellites are...broken?"

Scott rubbed at her temples, then she interlaced her fingers together on the desk. Miles saw then that what he'd mistaken for indifference or caution was actually exhaustion. She glanced up and looked at each of them, her gaze finally landing on Zeus.

Pulling in a deep breath, she asked, "Have you heard of the Kessler Event?"

Both Miles and Logan shook their head, but the words had an odd effect on Tanda. Her gaze had intensified as she stared across the room and out the windows.

Logan shifted forward in his seat, elbows on his knees, hands interlaced as if in prayer. "What is that? What is a Kessler Event?"

"Donald Kessler was a NASA scientist when he wrote a ground-breaking paper in 1978. He posited that the sheer amount of junk in orbit around the Earth had reached, or soon would reach, the point where it created a hazardous environment."

Miles felt as if he were back in medical school, striving hard to catch up, to understand a concept that was pivotal to his work. Only this, if it was what had happened, was pivotal to their lives. "Hazardous how?"

"Think of a very crowded freeway. The more cars, the higher the incidence of a collision."

"So...two satellites collided. Is that what you're saying?" Miles sat back, feeling relieved. There would be contingency plans for satellite failure. There would be back-ups. It might take days, even a few weeks, but eventually things would return to normal.

Scott was shaking her head. "Not just two."

"More than two?"

"Possibly...possibly all of them."

There was a stunned silence and then Miles, Logan, and Tanda all began speaking at once. Scott held up a hand to silence them.

"We don't know the answers to your questions. That's part of the problem. Kessler basically said—and I'm trying to simplify his theory which is actually quite complicated—he said that the more crowded the LEO becomes..."

"LEO?" Tanda shook her head. "What's LEO?"

"Lower Earth Orbit. Kessler said the more crowded it becomes, the more dangerous the entire situation becomes."

"Like the freeway." Miles was trying to envision the LEO, and all he could come up with in his mind was a scene from the movie *Gravity*. But that was a movie. It was Hollywood doing what Hollywood did best—being sensational and scaring the pants off movie goers who passed over their hard-earned money to experience a different life for a few hours. It wasn't real.

"So, what? There's been a giant pile-up..." He pointed a finger to the ceiling. "Up there?"

"More like high-speed collisions happening one after another. Remember, most satellites are travelling at speeds up to 28,000 kilometers per hour. Each collision would create more debris, which would in turn increase the chance of additional collisions. A virtual cascade of orbital debris."

"Hold up a minute." Tanda had pulled her attention back to them. She was in full police chief mode now, ready to interrogate. "How many satellites are we talking about?"

"That's a difficult number to calculate. We've launched over twelve thousand since 1957, and that number has been drastically increasing in the last few years. SpaceX alone has launched nearly two thousand. Starlink was in the process of deploying a broadband constellation that would consist of more than 40,000 craft."

"And all of the old stuff is still up there?"

"No. Many have been deorbited. Those either burned up on reentry or fell into the ocean."

"Except not all of it hits the ocean. There was a Russian space station—" Logan snapped his fingers. "What was the name of it?"

"The Mir. It weighed 286,600 pounds and most of it did burn up as it reentered orbit, but 1,500 fragments collided with the Earth's surface setting off sonic booms."

"So this is nothing new."

Scott sighed heavily. "Correct. The space shuttle Columbia in 2003, part of a Chinese rocket that very nearly hit New York City in 2020...there are over nine thousand tons of space junk above us and sometimes it comes down."

"But this time is different." Tanda waited until Scott looked at her directly. "It's worse."

"Yes."

"How much worse?"

"From what we've been able to document, which is limited given that all computers are off-line, the situation is catastrophic."

As Miles watched, Tanda's face blanched white.

He glanced at Logan, who was now studying the far wall. He seemed to be concentrating on putting the pieces of what Scott was saying together, trying to conceive what she was describing.

They'd come here for answers, but now that they were faced with them it only led to a hundred more questions and the unsettling feeling that things would never be the same again.

Chapter 17

T ANDA HAD VERY NEARLY lost her shit. When Scott first began talking, she'd felt the pressure of her position as police chief of Alpine collide with her responsibilities to her family. How would Abuela survive if this thing didn't have an end date? How would they all survive? She'd felt the air catch in her lungs, and it had been all she could do to breathe in and out. Not a panic attack, more like a reckoning with reality.

Then Scott had mentioned a "virtual cascade of orbital debris," and something about that phrase reminded her of Keme and his screenshots. She could vividly recall the video of the woman on the plane, terrified and panicked, just moments before her death.

"The planes crashed." Her words came out scratchy. Tanda cleared her throat, licked her lips, and tried again. "My brother, he caught a screenshot of a woman as her plane was going down over the Atlantic. Did they all... Did they all crash?"

"Most likely. There might have been a few that were able to land, but without GPS, without being able to speak to the control tower..." She shook her head. "Are you old enough to remember 9-11? Over four thousand flights were in the air when the FAA grounded every plane. That would have been impossible to do, to land them safely, were it not for radar, computer flight tracking, and communication. Two weeks ago, we didn't have any of those things."

When they only stared at her, Scott reached into her bottom desk drawer and pulled out a set of dominoes. Seeing Logan's look, she shrugged. "Things can get slow around here when you're waiting for a satellite to reposition so a scientist can view a different part of the galaxy. We've had more than one domino tournament in this room."

She began setting the dominoes up on end, evenly spaced apart, forming a circle. "Donald Kessler's paper suggested that we had reached a point of no return, if you will, regarding orbital satellites."

She now had created a complete circle, and Tanda couldn't have looked away if a clown in a rainbow wig had parachuted from a plane outside the window.

"His theory said that satellites were now so densely packed, if one were to lose its orbital controls and crash into another, what you'd have is a domino-type of effect. Each satellite would spiral into the next, eventually causing them all to fall out of orbit."

She touched one of the dominoes, and Tanda flinched, though she'd known what would happen. Hadn't every child played with dominoes in that way, seeing how many they could snake together and then knock down? The dominoes clattered onto Scott's desk, landing in a heap—a chaos of items.

"Scientists since Kessler have downplayed the possibility of such an event happening, but they all agreed on one thing. If and when collisional cascading begins, there would be no way to stop it."

Logan found his voice. "We wouldn't have the ability to stop it because our ability to communicate with those satellites still orbiting would likely be one of the first things to go."

Scott nodded.

Tanda flipped through Keme's screenshots in her mind. "Airlines were affected first."

"They wouldn't all have crashed at once. As they realized that they'd lost contact with the air controllers, as their screens went blank, they'd attempt to land, but..." She spread out her hands.

"Some would be over water." Logan sat forward, shoulders hunched. "Some would be over major metropolitan areas."

Miles put his hand on top of Zeus' head.

Tanda was still thinking of Keme's screenshots. "After that the news stations went off line—cable news, all of that."

"Yes."

"And finally, the stock market would take note." Tanda shook her head. "How would anyone still be able to trade?"

"Because all satellite capability didn't go out everywhere in the same moment. There was a lag depending on your location and which satellite your system was using."

"So what Keme saw was real?"

"I suspect so. There's a back-up power system for the New York Stock Exchange, for all monetary institutions, but they would no longer be able to communicate with one another. That's all dependent on 4G, which is dependent on satellite technology."

Tanda felt as if she couldn't breathe. She'd come to terms with what Keme had shown her, or she thought she had. But she hadn't really been able to envision such horror happening to every plane, on every highway, down every railroad track.

"Does the government, or the business sector, have a contingency plan for this?"

"No. A year after Kessler's paper was released, NASA did create an Orbital Debris Program. They made Kessler the head, but he retired in 1996. Others have tried to continue his work, but things have moved very quickly in the field of satellite deployment. The SSC..."

"Who?"

"Space Safety Coalition. They released a set of proposed voluntary guidelines."

"We all know how well voluntary guidelines work." Miles wiped at the sweat beading across his forehead, then rubbed his hand against his jeans.

"Exactly. And remember, this is a global problem involving many countries. There was even an idea to turn space junk into fuel by collecting it with a net or robotic arm."

"Probably had its budget cut," Logan murmured.

Tanda had to fight a sudden urge to laugh. Who laughed about the end of the modern age? She swallowed and fought to bring her emotions under control. "What does it mean...for the future? For tomorrow and next week and next year?"

"No one knows the answer to that question."

"Any clue as to whether this was a naturally unfolding event or whether it was caused?"

It was the first time Scott had hesitated. Like a professor attempting to convince a roomful of students, she'd laid it all out. Now she stopped, reached for a bottle of water, and took a long drink. Wiping the back of her hand across her mouth, she said, "My manners are terrible. You all must be tired and hungry. I'll take you down to our supply area."

But Tanda was on her feet, her eyes on the scene outside the window, on the sun dipping toward the western horizon. "We should go."

"That would be a very bad idea."

Tanda pivoted and faced the woman. "Why?"

"We have an excellent view from this vantage point. During the day, there's not much to see...same Texas landscape, birds and deer and the occasional fox going about their business." She stood and looked at each of them in turn. "Night is a different thing entirely. My advice would be that you start back early tomorrow morning."

"But Alpine is only..."

"I know how far Alpine is. You'll either have to go around Fort Davis or wait for one of Bennett's men to escort you through, and they hunker into a defensive position well before sundown. No one in, no one out. You'd be stuck between here and Fort Davis, and trust me...that would not be a wise move."

Something in Tanda bristled, but she nodded her head in agreement.

Scott led them down the hall and into a conference room. It looked more like a fall-out shelter. One end had been turned into a type of canteen. There were boxes of snack food, a cooler of drinks—no ice, of course—and a hand-lettered sign reminding everyone to

Help make supplies last.
Only take what you need.

Tanda had packed snack food and water in her backpack. She'd left Dixie's duffle in the Jeep. Logan also had a backpack, one half filled with vet supplies and the other half filled with food and jars of water.

He had jars of water.

How long had she worried about plastic bottles of water and their effect on the oceans, on the earth? Now it seemed that plastic bottles might be the last of their problems. It also seemed as if they wouldn't be seeing anything plastic for a long time. Miles had left his medical bag in the Jeep, but he'd also brought along a backpack. He crouched on the floor and removed two dog bowls from the pack.

Logan passed him a jar of water, and Miles poured it into one of the bowls. He poured a cupful of dog food into the other. Zeus waited for permission, then went straight to the water bowl, lapping it up as if he couldn't get enough.

The room's conference table had been removed. Instead, there were different types of chairs that must have been brought in from all over the facility—rolling office chairs, hard plastic chairs that probably came from the snack shop downstairs, and a few bean bag chairs that she guessed came from one of the college interns' apartments. They had the room to themselves. Scott had apologized, saying that she had a few things that had to be dealt with.

"I think she was being polite." Miles sank into one of the bean bag chairs, splayed his legs out in front of him, and stared up at the ceiling. "Giving us a little time alone..."

Tanda had looked longingly at a package of Famous Amos chocolate chip cookies, but she couldn't do it. Whoever was staying here would run out of food soon enough. She opened her pack, pulled out three granola bars, and tossed one to Miles and another to Logan. "So we can muse over how the world has ended?"

"Maybe." Logan grimaced. "That definitely was not good news."

"I don't like it. It's one thing if the satellites have all fallen. Okay, I can't do anything about that. But it's another thing entirely for law and order to have evaporated. Being afraid to drive after dark? For a forty-mile-trip?" She broke off a piece of the granola bar, but she didn't eat it. She simply stared at it. "Uh-uh. I don't like it."

She walked to the windows and stood staring out. All she could see was wave after wave of hills, shimmering in the Texas heat. It all looked so *normal*. It wasn't though. There wasn't a single thing that was normal about this. She thought about the small notepad in her pocket, resisted the urge to pull it out.

What Scott had told them changed everything.

She turned to study Logan and Miles.

Logan she had known for years. He was as solid and true as her brother, Keme. He could be trusted—to show up, to do the right thing, to pull his own weight as well as help others. He was that kind of person.

Miles she didn't know as well. She thought of that folder Stone had handed her detailing his previous life, the traipse up to his house with Stan Makowski, that view of the train wreckage from Old Ranch Road. And beneath all of that, running like an underground spring, the hope that he would be willing to put his grief aside and help. He had, or at least he was trying to.

She might not be able to get her mind and emotions around the situation they were in, but she could trust these two men, and that was as good a place as any to start.

They spent the next hour going over her list—amending, adjusting, adding. Tanda felt as if she had caught her second wind. They could do this. What other option did they have? They worked what they'd learned into her *Disaster Plan*, the name Logan gave her pocket notebook. They would fall into silence, then someone would come up with another item to be added, or one to be discarded, and off they'd go...trying to anticipate the future.

Trying to prepare their community for what was to come.

Various staff members wandered in and out of the conference room, smiling weakly, offering a slight wave, then selecting something from the food side of the room and disappearing back down the hall. Felicia appeared at one point and said that a smaller office down the hall had been set up for their use for the evening.

Dinner was rabbit stew with small potatoes and fresh carrots. They ate it outside, sitting around an inner courtyard, protected by the observatory walls but still able to see the sky, to feel the breeze on their face. Clouds had built up to the south as the sun set, and Tanda watched a continual display of lightning. Was Alpine receiving some much-needed rain? It did wonders to raise Tanda's spirits to think so.

"Who had the foresight to plant a garden?" Miles asked.

Scott grinned and pointed a spoon at a large man with a beard that reached to his chest. "That would be Jeremiah."

"Always enjoyed those prepper shows, you know? Some of the stuff is crazy…like the undead chasing people down the streets and secret government agencies making arks for humanity." Jeremiah took another spoonful of the stew and grinned. "But some of it, like planting a garden, made sense."

"We've since expanded Jeremiah's garden." This from a bespectacled man with a gray beard that looked rather new, as if he'd only recently given up shaving. "We should have done it sooner, but some of us—and I include myself in that group—were too busy looking at the stars. We didn't pay attention to what was happening around us."

He scraped the last bit of stew from his bowl, stared into it a minute, then directed his gaze above.

The courtyard was dark except for low-level solar lighting around the garden areas—areas which must have once held flowers but now held carrots, tomatoes, potatoes, even lettuce. It was a calming place, pushing back the horror of their reality. And the view of the stars was unlike anything Tanda had ever seen. She felt a bit dizzy staring up into that fathomless depth, as if her tether to Earth was tenuous at best.

Chapter 18

MILES DIDN'T HAVE TROUBLE accepting that the world had changed. It would have been harder if it had happened before—when he was in Houston, when his wife and daughter were alive, when he had people to worry about. Now it was just him and Zeus. Though that wasn't quite true. Tanda Lopez had worked her way under his defenses, and in Logan Wright, Miles recognized the potential for a type of friendship that was closer than a brother.

He could be in a much worse situation.

Maybe that was why the things Scott said earlier hadn't shaken him in any emotional way. It had, however, piqued his curiosity.

What exactly were they dealing with?

What was the forecast?

He cleared his throat, thanked them for the meal, then leveled his gaze on Shanna Scott. "I noticed you didn't answer our question when we were in your office—our question about whether the current situation is man-made or something else."

She gazed back at him, taking her time to answer. That was something he'd noticed about her earlier. She didn't jump in to fill a silence. Finally, she pushed her bowl away, then drank from her cup of water. When the silence was becoming awkward, she spoke.

"Honestly, we don't know. There are three possibilities. First, aliens—"

"You laugh," Jeremiah said. "But the U.S. Government was just beginning to open up about Unidentified Aerial Phenomena." He put the last three words in air quotes.

"The second possibility is that it was an act of war—say, China taking out one of our spy satellites."

"But the repercussions would affect everyone. They would be worldwide. Right?" Logan crossed his arms. "Would they take that sort of risk?"

"Many governments, including our own, are quite arrogant when it comes to how they perceive what they can set into motion, as well as what they can control." This from Felicia, who seemed way too young to know anything about world governments. Then again, everyone was beginning to look young to Miles. He understood this was a reflection of his age, not theirs.

Felicia sat forward, tucking her long auburn hair behind her ears. "It's conceivable that they—or we—thought it would be possible to take out one satellite without risking collisional cascading. Either way, it could have begun as an act of espionage or war and ended...well, ended with total annihilation of the satellite array."

"And the third possibility?" Tanda asked.

"What Kessler predicted—we unintentionally created a debris belt beyond what we could control."

"Does it matter?" This from an Asian post-doc student who had introduced himself as Jin. "Regardless how we reached this place, it's where we are."

"Hmm...sounds very Zen." Logan wriggled his eyebrows as he glanced first at Miles and then Tanda. Then he returned his attention to the group of scientists. "So your plan is to stay here indefinitely?"

"Here is as good as any other place," Felicia said. "And here we can still do what we're passionate about...study the stars."

"Even without power, there's much work that can be done," Scott added. "When the grid collapsed we had sixteen people here, including two visiting scientists. We're down to the five you see here, plus Bryce and Caroline who are on patrol."

"The others all chose to go home?" Tanda asked.

Felicia shared a look with Scott, who nodded once.

"I tried to leave," Felicia admitted. "Two days after the crash, I left with three other guys who thought they could make it to El Paso. We didn't get far. We didn't even make it to Van Horn. There was a roadblock across I-10."

Her hands had begun to shake. She clutched them in her lap and pushed through with the rest of her story. Zeus whined once, and Miles nodded his permission. The dog padded over to Felicia, sat next to her, pressed up against her side.

She put an arm around the dog, closed her eyes, then pushed on with her story. "We tried to turn around, but someone...one of those assholes with a semi-automatic weapon...started shooting. I don't know how they missed the tires or the engine block. Instead they shot out our windows—killing two of the guys I was with."

No one spoke for a minute, and then Tanda said, "I'm sorry that happened to you." The words were heartfelt and sincere, acknowledging the horror that this young woman had endured.

Miles realized that was the hardest part for Tanda—not living without the conveniences of modern society, but this quick descent into anarchy. She'd dedicated her life to law and order and now those things seemed no more tangible than a desert mirage.

"We came back here and buried our dead." Tears were sliding down Felicia's cheeks. She continued to pet Zeus, continued to share her story. "John decided to push on. He was trying to reach his family, but I'd seen enough. I chose to stay."

They continued talking for another hour. Part of the conversation was an attempt to come to terms with what had happened—like Felicia's description of the trip north. But some of it was sillier—wondering if the professional athletes were holed up in their mansions, if Neil deGrasse Tyson was explaining their current situation over a CB radio frequency, what all the avid tweeters were doing with their opinions. They listed what they missed the most—ice cream, music, e-books—and what they didn't miss at all—traffic and cable news and worrying about how to pay down their student debt.

By the time the Alpine group turned in to their room, Miles felt as if he'd been up for at least forty-eight hours. The fatigue was familiar, taking him back to his days as a resident at Good Samaritan Hospital in Cincinnati. It didn't matter that he didn't have a pillow, only a chair cushion and a light blanket from the gift shop that reminded him to *Preserve Dark Skies! See America* and sported the McDonald Observatory logo.

He fell into an immediate and deep sleep that wasn't broken until he heard Tanda and Logan zipping their supplies back into their packs. Zeus lay next to him, waiting, watching. Miles stood, stretched, and prepared to leave.

Fifteen minutes later they were loading their meager supplies back into their Jeep.

Only Shanna and Felicia were there to see them off.

"You can come with us," Tanda offered as she shook the young woman's hand.

"I'm not ready. Maybe...someday."

Tanda nodded as if she understood, then climbed into the front seat.

"Godspeed," Shanda said, which seemed an odd parting coming from a woman of science.

Perhaps not, though.

They were all cobbling together a new belief system in this post-modern world. At least that's how Miles had begun to think of it.

The first half of the drive back was uneventful. They were again escorted through the town of Fort Davis. Once they were through the other side of the barricade, they picked up speed. They passed the Chihuahuan Desert Research Center, which gave every appearance of being abandoned. Tanda had been trying the CB that

Keme had given her, and a static-filled voice had faded in and out twice.

"Can we pull over? Just...give me a minute," she said, slowly turning the dial on the CD receiver.

Logan pulled off where Kokernot Creek Road intersected with Highway 118. He exited the Jeep. Miles did the same. Zeus followed, relieving himself on the road sign.

Miles stared back in the direction they'd come, wondering if they should have tried to do more to help the people at the observatory. He was thinking of that, of what they'd hoped to learn and what they'd actually learned, of the people they'd met.

"Something's up with your dog," Logan said.

He turned to find that Zeus was on point, nose high, tail alert, muscles along the side of his body quivering. "What is it, boy?"

A whine escaped from Zeus, but he never took his eyes off the horizon to the northeast.

"I can't see anything," Logan said.

Miles moved to stand beside Zeus, looked intently in the same direction his dog was staring, but he couldn't see anything other than desert. "I'm not sure what he's spied. He's definitely locked on to something—maybe a rabbit or..."

"I'll grab the binoculars."

Logan returned with the binoculars and Tanda.

"What is it?" she asked.

"Maybe nothing."

But it was something. They all knew it was something. Zeus continued to whine. Logan scanned the distance, moving left to right, then right to left. Suddenly he jerked away from the binoculars, then looked again. "Get the medical bag. It's a person."

Tanda stayed with the vehicle. In normal circumstances they might have tried driving across the desert, but these weren't normal circumstances. A flat tire would be disastrous. Instead, Zeus led, while Miles and Logan did their best to keep up.

The man moving toward them, and Miles could now make out that it was a man, stopped when he became aware of their approach. He stood there in the middle of the desert—unmoving, definitely not calling out or waving for help. He reminded Miles for all the world of a rabbit, as if he were thinking that he could stay perfectly still and become invisible, as if he wished to simply fade into the desert.

When they were close enough to tell it was a man with his arm in a sling, Logan broke into a jog.

Zeus glanced back at Miles. "Yes. Go."

And then Zeus passed Logan. The dog barked only once, when he'd reached the man and stopped, holding his position until Miles and Logan could catch up.

"Quinton. Quinton Cooper." Logan stood with his hands on his knees, staring up at the man and trying to catch his breath.

"Wasn't sure who you were," Quinton admitted. "Wasn't sure if I should stay or run."

He was a large black man, probably six feet, and muscular. His arm was in a makeshift sling, and he wasn't sweating. It looked to Miles as if every drop of moisture in the man's body had dried and crystalized onto his skin. The milk jug he carried was empty, and he swayed slightly on his feet.

"We need to get him out of this sun," Miles said. Why hadn't he brought water with him? Because he hadn't actually believed they were running toward a man walking across the desert. "Can you walk to the Jeep?"

"I was planning on walking the rest of the way to Alpine. Walking to your Jeep shouldn't be a problem."

Still, he stumbled several times. When that happened, Miles reached out a hand to steady him. Quinton's skin was blazing hot. He would guess the man's temperature was 102, minimum. Zeus now tagged along at his side, as if having first spotted the man, he was now responsible for him.

As they approached, Tanda stayed at the Jeep, unwilling to leave it even for a moment. On seeing Quinton, she threw her arms around the big man. He winced slightly, though there was a huge grin on his face.

"Aren't you a sore sight to see, Tanda Lopez."

"The last I saw of you, you were taking two of the wounded from the train wreck to Fort Stockton. That was...over two weeks ago. What happened?"

Quinton leaned against the back seat, half in and half out of the Jeep, drinking from a thermos of water that Logan had pushed into his hands.

"Go slow with that," Miles reminded him.

"Miles is our doctor, and he's right." Logan added, "Don't want to rescue you just to kill you with too much water too fast."

Miles put a hand on Quinton's wrist, checked his pulse, and clocked it at north of one hundred. They needed to hydrate this man, get him lying down, and lower his body temperature.

"Quinton, I'm fairly sure you're suffering from heat stroke."

"Figured as much. That's why I was walking mostly in the late afternoon and evening. I'd sleep a little, then get up as soon as the sky lightened and walk again. Most days..." He rubbed at his head, then looked at Tanda and Logan as if he still couldn't believe they were real.

Miles suspected he had a splitting headache. A month ago, he would have already had an IV started, but he didn't have an IV with him, and even if he did...his inclination would be to save it. Hopefully they could slowly lower his body temperature with shade and water.

Miles removed an ace bandage from his medical bag, soaked it with water, wrung it out, then wrapped it around Quinton's head.

"Most days I would have stopped by this time. If I had, you wouldn't have seen me. I'd still be out there."

Miles checked his pulse again. It was still elevated, but not as much as it had been.

Logan squatted down in front of the man. "What happened, Quinton? Were you walking from Fort Stockton?"

"I was." He closed his eyes for a minute. "The two patients we were transferring died before we even arrived there, and perhaps that was a mercy."

"Why would you say that?" Tanda's voice was soft, worried.

"Because that town now resembles the seventh circle of Dante's *Inferno*."

He took another sip from the water, nodded at Logan that he understood to take it slow. Logan had taken a seat on the ground. Tanda stood closest to Quinton, as if to assure herself that he wasn't a mirage. Miles was standing, his arm over the open Jeep door, wondering when he should offer to reset Quinton's dislocated shoulder. For the moment, he seemed to need to relate the hell he'd lived through.

"What happened?" Tanda's voice was flat, as if she needed to steel herself against what he might say.

"No one knew what had happened—only that everything had stopped working. Cell service, internet, GPS—it was all out. I certainly didn't realize it was related to the train crash. We arrived at the emergency bay in Fort Stockton, transferred our two patients who were deceased. We were pretty intent on getting back to Alpine, like you had told us, to make another run." He shook his head and stared at the thermos of water. "They wouldn't let us leave. Said the road had been closed."

"This must have been...only a few hours after the train wreck."

"Exactly. I guess someone knew that it was more extensive than Wi-Fi outage. That afternoon I learned there had been three separate plane crashes near Fort Stockton and landlines weren't working. That was worrisome, but still...we couldn't wrap our minds around it."

"It's a satellite outage," Tanda explained. "As in all of the satellites."

"Oh." Quinton shook his head, pressed his fingertips against the bandage on his head.

"Do you want to lie down?"

Zeus had hopped into the back seat and was sitting pressed against Quinton.

Quinton looked at the dog, then at Miles. "Nah. I'm...I'm good—a little better, actually."

"Who is in charge in Fort Stockton?" Tanda asked.

"I don't know the answer to that. I never saw the man, though I heard a few people refer to him. Anyway, someone must have had an idea of what had happened because they didn't give a damn about our little train crash. We thought we'd be able to leave once things were straightened out, but one day turned into three and then they put razor wire around the city."

"Razor wire?" Logan stood, walked a few steps away and then back. "Why? And how? They enclosed the entire town of Fort Stockton?"

"They did. Armed guards commandeered all vehicles and all fuel. If you were leaving Fort Stockton, if you found a way through that razor wire—you were walking. Over eight thousand people in Fort Stockton, and they weren't letting anyone in or anyone out."

"Travis McKnight went with you—"

"Travis was determined to get back. The second night we were there he tried to take our ambulance, thought he could break through the perimeter they'd set up." He laughed but there was no mirth in it. "Never could tell Travis differently once he set his mind on a thing."

"What happened?"

"They shot him. Shot him through the window of that ambulance. I didn't see it, but they showed me later. Wanted me to know there was no leaving, that they wouldn't hesitate to kill anyone who tried."

"Why?" Logan asked. "Why would they even care?"

"I didn't understand that either, but I wasn't sticking around to find out. Two days after Travis was killed, I snuck out. Waited until four in the morning. My daddy always told me that was the best time to get away with something..." His bottom lip began to quiver, and he pulled it in, struggled for control over his emotions. Looking at Tanda, he asked, "My parents, are they all right?"

"They were yesterday when I left. I'm sure they still are."

"Okay. That's good. That's real good." He took another sip of the water.

Miles noticed that his hand was shaking badly now. His mental state was clear though. He wasn't slurring his words. Overall, he thought they had found him in time.

"I left on foot. Didn't take anything but this jug filled with water. I've been walking for..."

Logan shook his head in disbelief. "You've been walking for fourteen days."

"How did you survive?" Tanda waved toward the desert. "What did you eat?"

"Not much," he admitted. "I came across two cars on the road. Both were abandoned, guess they broke down. I found some food in those cars—leftover from someone's McDonald's stop, gum, even a box of granola bars." He glanced up and seemed to be suddenly aware that they were all three watching him. "Why do you suppose they'd leave that food there? Why didn't they take it with them?"

"People don't always act in logical ways when they're frightened." Miles had seen it before—when a hurricane was bearing down on them, when a tornado struck, whenever what was happening was beyond the mind's ability to put the pieces into a discernible whole. "It's...the back of the brain has taken over and it's telling them to flee."

"That's what I did." Quinton ran a big hand up and over his face. "That's what I did."

Zeus whined softly, turning his muzzle toward the big man, watching over him.

"I was afraid to sleep in those cars, afraid someone from Fort Stockton would be running patrols and would see me. That's why I didn't come down 67, which might have been faster. I knew they'd shoot me same as they shot Travis. So I just slept..." He waved toward the desert. "Out there. Middle of the day and middle of the night. Figured if a snake found me while I was sleeping and bit me, then it was my time to go."

His head dropped a little and he nearly spilled out of the Jeep.

"We need to get you back," Tanda said.

"Back to where?"

She exchanged a look with Miles and Logan. "Alpine. We're taking you back to Alpine."

"It's still there?"

"Yeah, Quinton. It's still there."

Miles stepped closer. "How about I take a look at that shoulder before we go?"

"Who are you again?" Quinton asked.

"Miles Turner, town doctor."

Quinton didn't look convinced until Tanda nodded her approval. Logan helped hold him steady, and Miles was able to pop the shoulder back into place with barely a peep from Quinton. By that point, he was swaying between sleep and wakefulness.

They all climbed into the Jeep and resumed their journey back home.

Chapter 19

T ANDA MIGHT HAVE FALLEN asleep. She blamed it on the warmth of the sunlight pouring through the Jeep's window, the lull created by the sound tires made on pavement, the fact that she'd tossed and turned much of the previous night.

She woke suddenly when she heard Logan gasp and the Jeep slowed.

When she opened her eyes, she couldn't quite believe what she was looking at. The town's medical center, the building where they'd housed patients who needed constant care, the place that had recently been staffed solely by nurses, was a charred debris.

No one in the Jeep spoke.

They all stared at the wreckage in horror.

And then Tanda remembered the lightning she'd watched the night before. Of course, it hadn't brought much needed rain. Had she seen a single water puddle? No. But the lightning had managed to start a fire and destroy their medical center. She shot straight through shock and depression and landed firmly on the side of unbridled anger.

She practically catapulted from the car.

Dixie was overseeing a crew of workers—some fire personnel, some citizens who had shown up to see what was burning.

"Tanda, you're back."

"Yeah." She stood there, hands on her hips, staring at the charred remains of the building.

She didn't even realize that the men were behind her until Dixie gasped, "Quinton..." and flew into the man's arms, nearly knocking him to the ground.

"Doc Logan picked me up on Kokernot Creek Road," Quinton explained. "What happened here?"

"Lightning strike. No water to fight it with, but we did manage to get everyone out safely."

Tanda knew it had nothing to do with their absence, but she couldn't help feeling that she had failed the town somehow. "What about the medical supplies?"

"Some were saved." Dixie's expression told Tanda all she needed to know—some, but not enough.

"The patients who were here?"

"All transferred to the nursing home in town. They...um...had enough beds." Dixie's eyes cut away.

Which meant that more had died. The combination of heat, inadequate medicine, and barely sufficient food was decimating their elderly population. Quinton's words echoed in her mind. *And perhaps that was a mercy...*

"We could use your help," Dixie said to Miles.

"Sure. What can I do?"

"Go through the building one last time to see if there's anything worth salvaging, anything we missed. I'll have one of my guys accompany you."

"Sounds good." He whistled once to Zeus, who bounded to his side.

Logan put a hand on Quinton's shoulder. "Let's get you to your parents."

"Do you want me to stay?" Tanda had no idea how she could help. What could she do that wasn't being done? It was as if the ineptitude of men and the fierceness of nature had combined to destroy them.

"Not necessary. We're good. You look like you could use some rest."

"I'm fine," Tanda snapped, then seeing the hurt look on Dixie's face, added, "Thanks for the bug-out bag. Your radiation detector came in handy. Come by my place tonight, and I'll tell you all about it. Logan and Miles, you too, if you're not too beat."

Both men said they'd be there.

"Do you want me to come by tonight, Tanda?"

"No, Quinton. Go home. Rest. Get hydrated. We need you here in Alpine, and it's wonderful to have you back, but take it slow, okay?"

The big guy nodded his head, though she wasn't sure how much he was taking in of what anyone said. He looked beat. He looked even more shell-shocked than she felt.

"Around seven?" Dixie asked.

"Sure."

Alpine itself looked the same as when they'd left it. Tanda breathed a sigh of relief that no other building had burned to the ground. By the time Logan dropped her off in front of the police station, she knew that she wouldn't be much good that afternoon. She was too tired. She had seen and heard too much. Her body had reached a tipping point, and it would crash if she didn't get some rest.

When she stepped into police headquarters, Edna nodded toward the back room. "Stan and Regina are back there trying to figure out what to do."

"About?"

"The mayor."

She heard raised voices and wondered what Melinda Stone had managed to stir up now. The room Edna motioned her toward was alternately called *the briefing room*, *the conference room*, or simply *the back*. It was barely large enough for a small conference table surrounded by six chairs. At one end of the room was a white board mounted on the wall next to a bulletin board.

"She's trying to tear us in two."

"We don't know that, Stan. We can't just push our way in and not expect some resistance."

"That's fine with me. I'd have no problem handling resistance because that's—"

Stan Makowski cut off what he was about to say when Tanda walked into the room. His complexion was red from his neck to his hairline, and sweat made his face shiny. As for Regina, she was standing at the board where they'd tacked a map of Alpine. Her hair was sticking out in several different directions, as if she'd been tugging on it in frustration.

"What's happened?" Tanda poured a glass of water from the pitcher on the table, then sank into a chair. "What has Melinda done?"

"Divided our town, that's what she's done."

"He's overstating it," Regina countered.

"Okay. You start, Regina. Give me your version while Stan gets some water."

He shot her a look, opened his mouth, thought better of it, then sank into a chair and also poured himself a glass of water.

"Melinda Stone and Ben Cason have apparently moved their office to one of the shops in the arts district."

"Moved their office?" Stan's fist came down hard on the conference table. "They took a quarter of our supplies and set up an encampment."

"We don't know they took a full quarter."

"We know she was spotted there yesterday afternoon in a truck, and after she left a quarter of our supplies were missing."

Tanda was too tired to shout over them. Perhaps that's what, in the end, caught their attention. Her voice, low and tired and filled with angst, caused Regina and Stan to stop talking and turn to look at her.

"I am very tired, and I need you two to focus. Be the professionals I know you are. Take a deep breath and talk to me."

Stan splayed his hands out in front of him on the table, as if he might need to sink his fingers through it and hold on.

Tanda remembered ordering that table. It had been two years ago, and they'd ended the year with a little extra money in their budget. The table was oval and dusty gray. The black leather and chrome chairs offered lumbar support. Had that really once been important to her?

"Chief, are you okay?" Regina sat next to Stan.

They both waited for her to speak. She did, finally, haltingly. She didn't give them the details, said she'd brief everyone the following day, but she laid out the shape of the thing. Satellites were down, would stay down for a very long time. Fort Davis and Fort Stockton had both set up perimeters. They couldn't expect help. They needed to be prepared to defend Alpine and its citizens. They needed to begin preparing for winter—now.

Regina looked stunned.

Stan simply stared at his hands. Was he thinking about his children? His wife? Their unborn baby?

"Now tell me, calmly and succinctly, about Melinda."

She'd moved her office, taken some of the supplies, pulled those who were loyal to her close. She hadn't made contact, no announcement of any sort. Ben Cason had been seen with her.

"I think we should just give her a little time and space to cool off."

"And I think we should go in and take back what belongs to this town."

"Okay." Tanda stood, walked to the map, and studied the few streets that they considered the arts district. She picked up a red marker and uncapped it, addressing Regina and Stan as she tried to assess what they were facing. "Where, exactly is she?"

Stan cleared his throat, which sounded a bit hoarse from the shouting match he'd had with Regina. "As far as we can tell, south of 67 from S. Halbert Street to 5th."

Tanda drew a red circle around the area. It was a fair portion of the downtown area, but she couldn't see that it was strategically important. She didn't know why the mayor had chosen that section of town, other than the fact that it was the location of the homes and shops of her strongest supporters. It was a gentrified part of one of the oldest sections of Alpine. Artists had moved there from Taos and Santa Fe and Sedona. Some had come from as far as northern California looking for cheaper land, lower taxes, and a conducive space to create and sell their art.

They didn't understand ranchers, and ranchers didn't understand them. The fact that Melinda Stone had won the last election by a good ten percent attested to the fact that the art community's numbers were growing.

"We need to keep our distance and remember she is the mayor."

"We need to deal with her swiftly and definitively."

"You're both right," Tanda finally said. "We need to give her a little space and time, and we need to take back what the people of this town—*all* the people of this town—will need."

She capped the marker and dropped it in the little silver tray that abutted the white board. "I'll go and see her tomorrow morning."

"What do you want us to do until then?" Stan's voice was tired.

Could a voice be tired? Tanda thought it could. She thought he was nearly as weary as she was. "Do your job, work your shift, and then go home."

"But—"

"Go home, Stan. Go home to your family and let me handle this."

Regina looked as if she wanted to argue, but she didn't.

Tanda exited the room, stopped by her office, and scribbled a short list of names on a sheet of paper, then she stopped by Edna's desk and handed the paper to her. "Contact everyone on that list, and have them at my apartment at seven tonight."

"You've got it, Chief."

And then she walked out of the office, went home, and slept, pausing only long enough to set the alarm on her wind-up clock.

Chapter 20

MILES LEFT ZEUS AT the office. He wasn't sure how many people would be at Tanda's, and his dog seemed exhausted. He fed him a full cup of dog food and tried not to worry that his supply was dwindling.

He walked to Tanda's apartment, and when he stepped into the room, he had a moment of unexpected clarity.

When Stella and Mae were killed, he'd wondered why he was still alive. Many nights, he'd wished that he had died with them. What was the point in living in a world without the two people who mattered most? Why was he still there? His single wish for the three years since that fateful day had been that he might join them.

As he took a seat on the floor, his back against Tanda's bookcase, he understood why his wish hadn't been granted. This was why. These people were why.

He was needed here, and the people around him—they were good people. The ache in his heart, the overwhelming loss, was as fierce as it had been the first night when the police officer had knocked on his door. He supposed it always would be.

He thought of the famous Leonard Cohen line. Something about everyone being broken, about accepting the cracks in our lives, because the cracks were how the light got in.

As he sat there, nodding at friends and waiting on Tanda to begin this impromptu meeting, he felt that light, felt its warmth inside of him. It didn't banish the loss, but it co-existed somehow.

"Thank you for coming." Tanda looked better than she had standing outside the ruined hospital. Dark circles still rimmed her eyes, but her posture was better, her voice was stronger.

"I think everyone knows everyone." When Miles raised his hand, she smiled. "Everyone except the new guy...Miles, you've met Ron, Dixie, and Emmanuel."

"I have."

"Keme is my brother, and Lucy is my sister-in-law."

He nodded at the couple sitting across from him, even as he wondered why they were in attendance. Everyone else, except for an older gentleman and Logan, seemed to be a city employee.

"And this is Jackson Castillo, rancher extraordinaire."

Jackson nodded a greeting, but he didn't smile or wave or acknowledge Tanda's words in any way. The man looked as if he'd been carved from a saddle—a very old, well-worn saddle.

Tanda outlined what they'd learned at the observatory. She ended with, "So basically what we've been calling *the collapse* should actually be *the collision*. Not that the name of the thing matters. Am I missing anything? Logan, Miles, you were both there."

"I'd say you've summed it up well." Logan was also sitting on the floor, his legs stretching in front of him and crossed at the ankles. "The scientists at the observatory were certain as to what had happened, but they couldn't confirm how or why. As far as how long the outage would last, they weren't sure of that either, but they suspected it would be years at the very least."

No one spoke. Tanda allowed a moment of silence for the information to sink in. Finally, she looked at Lucy and waited.

Lucy's eyes were somber, but she smiled slightly. "*This is the way the world ends. Not with a bang but a whimper.* T.S. Eliot penned those words in 1925, but they seem written for such a time as this."

Glancing at Miles, Keme explained, "Literature professor. She has a quote for any occasion."

"I can always count on Lucy to help put things in perspective." Tanda glanced at Miles, her eyebrows raised.

Funny how well he understood that expression.

Logan cleared his throat. "I would add that the situation in Fort Davis and Fort Stockton raises grave concerns."

Tanda quickly filled everyone in on the perimeter surrounding Fort Davis, finding Quinton Cooper walking across the desert, and what he had been escaping from at Fort Stockton.

"I'd like to say I'm surprised, but I'm not." Jackson spoke matter-of-factly. "When there's a vacuum of any sort, something fills it. In this case, the hole left by the absence of technology was filled by..."

"Assholes. I think the word you're looking for is assholes." Dixie looked serious, but her words eased the tension in the room.

It was what it was, Miles realized—a sentiment he'd always considered worthless and cowardly. Now he understood that those words modeled simple acceptance, which was the only way to move forward.

"We need a long-term plan," Tanda continued. "And we need it tonight. But before we start on that, I want to tell you about Melinda Stone and Ben Cason."

No one was surprised, but Melinda's abdication—if that's what it was—added another layer of complication to their current crisis.

Tanda pulled her now worn notebook from her pocket. She'd smiled when Logan had called it her *Disaster Plan*. Miles had seen her scribbling in it often, and of course their late-night brainstorming at the observatory had been recorded there as well. He had always been a fan of using the NOTES feature on his phone, but he supposed those days were over for the foreseeable future.

"I've tried to group my concerns together, and by the time we're finished I think you'll understand why you're each here."

The growing rift between the ranchers and artists was her first concern. Jackson assured her that while the men he knew weren't exactly cozy with the artists in town, neither did they have time to harass them. "You know these men as well as I do, Tanda. It's hard enough to make a living without adding a political feud to your daily chore list."

"We still aren't sure who threw the first punch at the park," Lucy pointed out.

"True, and it could have been one of the ranchers. We're all exhausted and, if I were honest, a little frightened. Still, throwing a punch is one thing, coming to town in order to break into an art shop..." He shook his head once, definitively. "That isn't happening."

Tanda was insistent that they bridge the gap between the two groups. Since Lucy was a literature professor at Sul Ross, she was the obvious choice.

"I'll see what I can do."

Her next item was coming up with a group of riders who could monitor the perimeter of their town. "I'm not sure we want to fence it off—not yet, but we want to know what's happening. We want to know what's headed our way before it gets here."

Jackson sat forward. "I'd suggest you put Dylan in charge of that."

"Dylan Spencer?" Tanda didn't bother to hide her surprise. "He's been a pain in my ass since he threw the touchdown that won the state playoffs."

Ron and Emmanuel both smiled at that.

"Good game though," Ron pointed out.

"The boy can throw a ball," Emmanuel added.

"He's changed, Tanda." Jackson kneaded one hand with the other. "I know it's only been two weeks, but Dylan's been meeting with other kids his age. They haven't exactly waited around for us to tell them where they're needed."

"It's true," Ron said. "Dylan and a few of his friends—guys and girls—helped deliver water last week."

"They also showed up to help with the fire." Dixie was nodding her head. "I think it's a good idea."

"Well, color me surprised, but then that's why I pulled you all together. You know things that I don't."

It seemed to Miles that the mood in the room had shifted. They'd gone from a group that was confronting an unfathomable problem to people who just might be able to cobble together a plan.

"What about using some of the Sul Ross students to check on the elderly?" Miles stretched his neck to the left then right, hearing a satisfying pop. "Anyone who was in a science- or health-related major could work at the nursing home and in my office. It's not a bad idea to give them experience now, before it's needed."

Emmanuel had pulled out his own pad and begun taking notes. "We still have quite a few nurses, too—we could rotate the students through the nursing home, learning under the nurses' supervision, then assisting you."

Tanda held up a hand. "Remember that Miles is only in town Monday through Wednesday, so let's work around that."

"No, I'm not."

They all turned to look at him, but he didn't even hesitate. "Until this crisis has passed, my little cabin on Old Ranch Road is going to have to wait."

Tanda smiled, but Logan pointed out, "Then we're going to need to find you somewhere to sleep other than that office."

"Which brings us to the topic of homes—quite a few are now empty." Dixie sat forward, elbows on her knees, fingers interlaced. "Some people were out of town when this thing happened. Other families were driving through and have been stuck living at the hotel—which isn't ideal."

"I won't requisition someone's home."

"No. I wasn't thinking of that, but an empty home is more likely to be vandalized. We could temporarily relocate some folks to those homes, explain the conditions for their using it. Also, if there are people living outside of town who want to come in, we should let them."

"With the understanding that they are only caretakers of the property."

"Yeah. Our own Alpine Apocalyptic Air B&B system."

Which brought more nods of approval.

"What about fuel and generator power? Someone needs to find out who has some, how much they have, and if they're willing to share."

Keme raised his hand. "I'll do it."

Miles was beginning to think they could do this, and he was understanding the wisdom of including the people that Tanda had invited to the meeting. She hadn't brought her officers or Dixie's fire personnel. She wasn't trying to win an argument. She was trying to solve a problem, and it was going to take every one of them...hell, every person in Alpine, if they were going to survive.

Logan sat back, his hands interlaced behind his head, his gaze on the ceiling. "What are we going to do about our drug and alcohol abusers? Take care of that problem, and you go a long way toward making this town a cohesive group."

"Locking them up isn't the answer," Tanda said. "I had to let Owen Bradley go. There was no way I was keeping him in a jail cell in this heat."

"Wait." Jackson raised a hand. "It's been two weeks. Wouldn't they already be dried out, or whatever you call it?"

"Not necessarily." Logan crossed his arms. "I suspect we had enough liquor and drugs in town to get them through the first ten, maybe fourteen days."

"But now we're at day eighteen." Keme shook his head. "Maybe that explains your rise in vandalism, Tanda."

"Maybe so."

"I've had a few come to me begging for something, anything that might help," Logan admitted. "I didn't have anything to give them."

"What can we do to help?" Tanda asked.

Logan nodded toward Miles with a smile. "Ask him."

"Basically we try to manage their discomfort. Mind you, this isn't like being in rehab where we could use methadone or Naloxone. But we also don't have to worry about relapse. Drug availability has dried up like everything else."

"Is there anything we can do?" Lucy asked.

"The most common side effects of drug or alcohol withdrawal include anxiety, insomnia, general discomfort, and mood swings. My suggestion would be to pick a location where we can put these people together and have medical personnel there at all times."

"Could we use Sul Ross students?" Logan asked.

"It might work, as long as we had a nurse, you, or myself to supervise."

"How about housing them at the Maverick Inn?" Emmanuel tapped his fingertips against his knees. "JoAnn's been asking how she can help."

"Pretty swanky place for drug addicts," Dixie said.

"I like it." Tanda tapped a pen against her pad. "There's a courtyard there where they could get some fresh air. It's also close enough to downtown that Miles or Logan can check in once a day."

"I'll talk to JoAnn first thing tomorrow."

"What else?" Tanda asked. They'd been talking for over an hour, but if anything she looked more energetic.

It occurred to Miles that she'd been carrying all of this around in her head, tossing it about and trying to find solutions. Having a group of people she trusted was spreading out the burden, lightening her load.

"I don't like our supplies being so far from the center of town." Ron let his gaze drift around the group. "I also don't like Melinda knowing where they are."

"We could move them," Emmanuel offered. "Somewhere on campus maybe? Somewhere she wouldn't think to look."

They batted around ideas and finally settled on the Admin building of Sul Ross. Lucy would check and see if any administrators were on campus to approve the plan. If not, they'd simply use the space and apologize later.

"I'll put a couple of my officers on it tomorrow," Tanda said.

Dixie nodded. "And a few of my firefighters can help as well."

"We'll get it moved. What else?"

"I'm concerned about what medications we have and don't have." Miles steepled his fingers together. "People aren't going to want to give up what they have, and the pharmacies are probably emptied out."

"Some of our elderly population is just plain frightened." Lucy ran a hand through her hair, then pulled it over her shoulder. "What about Pastor Tobias? Maybe he could help."

"Good idea, Lucy." Tanda nodded. "Can you speak to him?"

Lucy nodded and the room grew quiet.

Ron ran a hand over his nearly bald head. "Let's have a city-wide meeting tomorrow, explain it to our residents."

Jackson agreed. "We have good people here in Alpine. They'll see the wisdom in it. What they want is information and a plan from people they trust. That was the problem with Melinda—no one really trusted her."

"Speaking of our mayor, what's our play there?" Logan said what they'd all been thinking. "She's not going to go away quietly."

"She doesn't have to go away though." Tanda had obviously given the subject of Melinda Stone a lot of thought. "She can stay where she is. Hell, the entire art community can stay in their corner of Alpine if they want, but we need to make it clear that if they don't contribute..."

"If they put nothing into this town, then they get no help from this town." Jackson's voice had turned hard. "That's non-nego-tiable. What we're facing, the coming months and years are going to be the hardest that any of us have ever faced. We can help those who are weaker or older, but we can't help anyone who refuses to actively participate in the preservation of this town."

Which seemed to nicely sum up what they were facing.

After that the meeting began to break up.

Miles held back, until it was just Tanda, Logan, and himself. It wasn't that he thought of the three of them as the leaders of post-modern Alpine. It was more that he was concerned.

"When will you go see Stone?" Logan asked.

"First thing tomorrow."

"Would you like one of us to go with you?" Stone hadn't seemed like a violent person to Miles, but then who could tell these days? Pushed into a corner, he suspected anyone could react with extreme measures. And although Melinda Stone hadn't been pushed anywhere, she'd willingly placed herself in a position that seemed to have no exit.

"I'll take Stan with me."

There seemed to be nothing else to say. As he and Logan were leaving, Miles turned back. "Can I give you some free medical advice?"

"Well, since it's free..."

"Get some rest. If you're having trouble sleeping try deep breathing or maybe read some of that poetry your sister-in-law seems to like. Anything that will help your brain to slow down."

"Sure thing, Doc." She rolled her eyes, then put a hand on his shoulder. "I appreciate your concern."

Miles followed Logan out into the darkness.

"Guess you'll be moving tomorrow."

"I guess I will."

"Never thought of yourself as a townie, I'll bet."

"I didn't, Logan. But then a lot of things are happening that I never envisioned."

Which seemed to be the understatement of the night. They walked in silence until they reached his office.

"What concerns me isn't all that stuff we mentioned tonight," Logan admitted. "It's the things we haven't thought of yet."

And that seemed to sum up their situation perfectly because what they hadn't thought of could be the thing that killed them.

Chapter 21

THE REST OF THE week passed in a whirlwind. Tanda should have felt exhausted, but her weariness had dropped away. On Thursday morning, she took Regina with her to see Melinda Stone because Stan was home with Zoey. Her labor had begun, but the contractions were far apart. He promised to let her know if that changed.

Tanda and Regina met with Ben Cason because Melinda refused to see them. The meeting itself lasted less than ten minutes.

Melinda was not abandoning her post as mayor.

She was regrouping.

They claimed to know nothing about missing supplies.

She'd be in contact.

"What are you going to do?" Regina asked as they walked away.

"What can I do? I can't make her come out. Seems to me that we get on with preparing for other threats. We do what we can."

Supplies were moved to Sul Ross.

Students volunteered to maintain a rotating watch.

Their group of young interns swelled to two dozen.

What addicts they could find were moved to the Maverick Inn. Tanda's niece, Akule, offered to coordinate volunteers who would help those detoxing. When she met with Tanda and asked to be assigned there, something in her manner suggested to Tanda that she'd dealt with drug withdrawal personally, or maybe she'd been close to someone who had. Either way, Tanda was happy to see the young woman step up.

Emmanuel Garcia agreed to coordinate the health checks for seniors and those who were disabled. Ron Mullins matched up vacated houses with people who had been sheltering in the local hotels. Dixie Peters and a few of her personnel visited homes outside the town limits. Only a third of those people accepted the offer to move into town which was more than Tanda had expected.

They were so busy that they put off the town meeting until Friday night. They needed time to get word out anyway. Everyone who could attend, should attend.

She was worried about Melinda and Ben.

She shouldn't have been.

Friday morning, Gonzo showed up in her office to inform her that the two of them were gone. "Left with a couple families, took all the supplies and went west."

"To Marfa? That's a surprise." She sat back and studied the man in front of her.

Gonzo Watson looked quite different from the man who had very nearly started a riot ten days earlier. He still sported a somewhat scraggly beard, but his long hair was neatly combed and pulled back in a band.

"Look, I'm afraid you and I got off on the wrong foot."

Tanda waited.

"What I mean to say is that I'm sorry." He combed his fingers through his beard. "I suppose I arrived in Alpine with something of a chip on my shoulder, and Melinda Stone, well, she's a woman who likes to stoke a small flame into a full-fledged fire."

He held up his hands, palm out. "Not that I'm blaming her. I simply chose the wrong side of things. I let my past experiences cloud my judgement."

"So you're here because…"

"Because I want to know how I can help. And you might not believe that. I wouldn't blame you. But I could have left with Stone and Cason. Truth is, if these are my last days, I want to spend them fighting on the right side."

Which was good enough for Tanda. She stood, shook his hand, and said, "Edna has a list of jobs that need to be done."

He'd made it to the door when he turned around. "I'm not the only one. Left in the artist community, I mean. They're a little more tentative. Weren't sure what kind of response they'd get. What should I tell them?"

"Tell them that anyone who is willing to work is welcome. Tell them we need every man, woman, and teenager who will help."

Which brought the first smile to the old guy's face that she'd seen.

The day was going well, too well, when Lucy appeared at her office door. "It's Abuela. She's dying, Tanda."

Tanda thought she must have misheard, or maybe Lucy was referring to someone else's *abuela*. "My *abuela*?"

"Yes."

"But I was just there a few days ago."

"She took a sudden turn for the worse. She asked for you."

"Right. Of course." Tanda's mind had frozen. She was literally incapable of thought, but then her gaze landed on a family photo that she kept on her desk—a photo of her and Keme and Abuela when Tanda was no more than ten years old. The old woman had always been a part of her life. She'd always been a steady, guiding light. "We'll pick up Miles on the way."

Lucy stopped her with a shake of her head. "Keme's already doing that, but..."

"But what?"

"She's refusing any extreme measures, and your parents agree."

From anyone else those words would have sounded insane, but Tanda knew her grandmother better than that. If she thought now was her time, she would insist on doing it on her terms.

They took Tanda's personal vehicle and picked up Akule on the way. It felt strange to be driving again, and she probably should have saved the gas, but she needed to be there as quickly as possible. She didn't want to miss saying goodbye. By the time she reached her parents' home, Keme was already there with Miles.

He met her at the car. "Her pulse is quite low. She's not in any pain that I can tell."

She nodded, tears blurring her vision. "Is it her diabetes?"

"Hard to say. Maybe a combination of things. Or maybe it's just her time."

Abuela was lying in her bed. She looked smaller, looked like a child lying there beneath a lightweight quilt. The window was open and a light breeze stirred the air. Still it seemed oppressively hot to Tanda.

Her mother had been sitting on the bed beside Abuela. She stood when Tanda walked into the room, patted the spot she'd vacated. Tanda sat there. Akule stood next to her. Tanda reached for her grandmother's hand, held it, stared at it. Abuela's hands, like her person, were small, weathered, thin. Evidence of a life lived for many years, through many tragedies.

"It's been good," Abuela said, opening her eyes. "My life, it has been very good."

Tears slipped down Tanda's cheeks. She made no attempt to wipe them away. There was so much she wanted to say to this woman, and now there was no time.

"I love you, Abuela. I will..." The words clawed to escape from her throat. "I will miss you so much. We will all miss you so very much."

Abuela smiled. "Every ending is a beginning, Tanda Kaliska."

She closed her eyes then, and she didn't speak again. Tanda and Keme, Miles, Lucy and Akule, her mother and father stayed there, wanting to help in some way, wanting her to not feel alone.

The sun beat down outside the window, the breeze continued to ruffle the curtains, and then, as gently as a bird taking flight, she was gone.

Four hours later, Stan's baby girl was born.

Chapter 22

MILES WAS WITH TANDA when her grandmother breathed her last, and he was with her when Stan Makowski placed his baby girl into her arms. "You'll be her Godmother?"

"Of course. Of course I will."

She looked up, met Miles' gaze, and smiled.

Later, as they were walking back to her apartment, he said, "You've been through a lot today. Maybe you should take tomorrow off."

"I don't think there are any vacation days during the apocalypse."

He didn't laugh, didn't even smile. "I'm serious, Tanda. You're not superwoman."

"Ouch."

He bumped his shoulder against hers.

"Abuela would have liked the symmetry of it...little Chloe being born on the same day that she passed. That's how we think of it. A passing from this life to the next."

"Do you believe that?"

"I have no idea what I believe. Do you?"

"I want to. When my wife and daughter died, my belief system—fragile as it was—sort of tanked. Now, I don't know."

It was the most he'd ever shared, and something about uttering the words relieved some of the pressure in his chest.

"Did you see how much hair Chloe had?"

"Pretty, too. She looks like her mother."

They stopped outside Tanda's apartment.

"Want to come up?"

"Better not. You look ready to drop here on the sidewalk."

"Thanks?"

He laughed. "I wanted to tell you that Akule is doing a wonderful job at the Maverick Inn. And Lucy has really stepped up with the Sul Ross students."

"Keme's pretty optimistic about our amount of fuel reserves."

"You have a good family."

Tanda smiled and the strain of the day seemed to melt away. "Have you moved yet?"

"Soon." He hesitated, then asked, "Meet me on the green across next to the courthouse in the morning? I'll bring coffee."

"You've got a deal. First light."

And then she was gone.

Miles walked home, fetched Zeus and took him on a short walk, then bedded down on the cot in his office. He wouldn't mind being in an actual house with an actual bed, but considering why it was vacant turned his thoughts to all that had happened since the day of the train crash.

Some people had left. Others had simply been caught out of town. Would any of them ever return? He could have spent hours batting that one around, but for once his body won over his mind and he fell into a deep and much-needed sleep.

He woke to a banging on his office door. The sky was still dark, but there was the barest hint of light to the east.

Dylan Spencer stood there, turning a well-worn cowboy hat in his hands. "It's the mayor. We found her."

Zeus pushed past Miles, walked to the green patch of grass separating the sidewalk from the street, and relieved himself.

"Found her?"

"She's, uh...she's dead."

"Dead."

"Tanda asked me to fetch you."

Which woke him up immediately. "Let me grab my medical bag." The kid could be wrong. It was possible there was something he could do.

"You won't need that," Dylan said.

"You're sure?"

"Yeah. I'm sure."

Dylan explained they'd found her on their four o'clock patrol, which meant that someone had wanted them to find her. Otherwise the darkness would have cloaked her body. She was just past the patrol line on the west side of town. She'd been knifed in the stomach and there was duct tape affixed to her hands and mouth.

"Why duct tape her if you're going to kill her?" Miles asked.

Tanda shook her head. "It might not have happened that way."

"What do you mean?"

"She wasn't killed at another location and dumped here. Whoever did this..." Tanda followed the faint trail of blood for thirty feet.

Where it stopped, Miles could just make out tire tracks.

"They did it here. Look at the blood trail. Clearly extends from here, where a vehicle parked...to there, where her body was found."

"And the duct tape?"

"We can't know for sure, but it could be that they taped her mouth so no one would hear her crying for help."

"It's possible," he admitted. "With a stomach wound it depends on what was punctured. It might have taken several minutes for her to bleed out."

Tanda's expression was grim. "And yet they wanted her found. Clearly this is supposed to be a message or warning of some sort."

Later that afternoon, Miles looked up from his desk to find Logan standing in the doorway with two men who were sunburned, exhausted and swaying on their feet. He poured them each a cup of water. "Better sit down before you fall down."

"The patrol picked them up outside the perimeter on the east side of town," Logan explained.

"We're from Marathon," the larger of the two men said.

Miles studied them, trying to assess their condition. "That's a good thirty miles. Isn't it?"

Logan nodded.

The slimmer, slighter man was sipping water as Miles had instructed. "We biked it."

"Motorcycles?"

He shook his head. "Ten speed."

The big man was Cameron Boyd. The smaller was Gregory Hunt. Miles wished that he could be surprised at the story that spilled out of the two guys, but he wasn't sure if anything would ever surprise him again. They were married in a civil ceremony in Little Rock Arkansas. Cameron was a chef. Gregory was a wannabe writer. They'd moved to Marathon because the pay was good and they'd needed a change.

"Got a little more of that than we planned for." Gregory was no more than five foot, eight inches and had a scholarly air about him.

Miles would have pegged him for a writer in his first three guesses. Lucy would have given him a lot of grief for that. She probably would have rolled out a list of male novelists and poets built like linebackers.

"No one could have foreseen..." Cameron waved out the window to the now empty street. "This."

Miles leaned against the exam room's counter top, waiting for the rest of their story.

Logan had pulled up a chair, turned it around, and straddled it. "Why don't you tell us exactly what happened in Marathon."

"People's true colors came out. That's what happened." Gregory sipped from his cup of water and stared at the floor.

When his partner continued to gaze into his cup, Cameron spoke up. "At first, after the collapse of whatever, everything seemed fine. For a day, maybe two. It was kind of a joke, everyone laughing about needing to take a digital detox anyway."

"By the third day, things got ugly."

"The owner of my restaurant disappeared. He just slipped away, got into his jet, and was gone. No warning. No instructions."

"That's when the threats started."

"Threats?" Miles glanced at Logan. "What kind of threats?"

"The usual. Graffiti on our car. *Fags aren't wanted here*, that sort of thing."

"The dead coyote was placed on our doorstep the end of that first week. Gutted and stinking."

"We decided we had to leave. Started trying to pull together some supplies."

"Quietly of course." Gregory glanced up. "We're not fools."

"Then some friends of ours, a lesbian couple, were killed."

"Killed? You're sure it was murder?" Logan was studying the two closely.

"Yeah. We're sure." Cameron's right hand had begun to shake. He set the cup of water on the table. "Jim Ferguson pulled them out into the middle of the street and shot them."

"Which was when we decided we couldn't outrun them in our Miata."

"We took the bikes instead."

"Rode at night, hid during the day. Marathon is running patrols, picking up anyone they come across."

"We'd heard things were bad in Fort Stockton, so we headed here. Alpine was...it was the only other choice."

Gregory seemed to draw himself up. "The thing is that we don't intend to go through what happened in Marathon again. If we're not welcome here, we'll keep going."

"Greg..."

"We've talked about this, Cameron. It's better to know up front."

Miles looked at Logan and wasn't at all surprised when he smiled.

"If you're willing to work, you're welcome."

And it really was as simple as that. Miles wanted to think that this little town set on a high plateau in the Chihuahuan desert was inclusive and kind. And perhaps they were. Certainly, some of them were. But the truth of the matter was that they needed every able-bodied person they could get. Miles had the sense that a battle was looming, and he could only hope they had enough people to win it.

By the time the town meeting was held that night, the Alpine grapevine had taken care of spreading the details of recent events. No one was surprised when Tanda told them about Melinda Stone. Everyone had even heard about the two guys from Marathon and why they were there.

The entire group that had been in Tanda's apartment was sitting on the gazebo stairs. Tanda updated the crowd on what they'd learned at the observatory. Then, one by one, each addressed the crowd, outlining the conservation methods that would need to be put in place. Water would be the most critical item. By the time summer rains came, they needed to have cisterns in place. Put out anything that could catch water. In the meantime, the ranchers who had wells and springs were willing to share. It wouldn't be enough for long baths and watering lawns, but it would see them through. No one would die of thirst.

It was critical that everyone plant a garden.

Medicine would be pooled and distributed by Miles and Logan. The perimeter around Alpine would be tightened. "We won't restrict people from going through," Tanda clarified. "But neither will we let them take what we need for the people of Alpine."

Miles couldn't help comparing this town meeting to the earlier one. There were no fist fights this time.

Everyone was in agreement.

Only two things surprised Miles.

The nine people who had met in Tanda's apartment two nights earlier were unanimously voted in as The Council—an idea proposed by the old police chief's wife, Mrs. Crowder, and seconded by Quinton Cooper.

The second surprise did much to assuage Miles' fear that the townspeople didn't fully understand their situation. They wanted a battle plan. They wanted to be prepared. It was determined that there would be four main groups. People were assigned to the group that was on their quadrant on the map. They would drill. They would plan. And they would be ready for whatever was coming their way. Or at least they'd try.

Chapter 23

A WEEK PASSED, AND the townspeople settled into a rhythm. Tanda was proud of how they'd responded.

She didn't know exactly what lay ahead, but she felt confident that they were doing everything possible to prepare for it. She started sleeping better, rising early, sharing the first cup of coffee with Miles.

On Monday morning, Tanda slumped onto the park bench across from city hall. Miles was already there, with Zeus lying at his feet. Miles picked up his thermos, poured coffee into an extra mug he'd brought and passed it to her.

She smiled her thanks, smelled deeply of the brew before taking the first sip. "I'm going to miss coffee."

He laughed and sipped from his own mug. "We're not the first generation to deal with that. During the Great Depression and both world wars, people used all manner of things to make coffee. Acorns, even pecans."

"Look around, Miles. Do you see any pecan trees?"

"We'll figure it out."

He bumped his shoulder against hers, and Tanda felt marginally better—until the image of Melinda Stone flashed into her mind.

"I keep thinking about Melinda Stone. I never liked the woman, but she didn't deserve that. No one deserves that."

"You couldn't have stopped it."

Instead of answering, she pulled two granola bars out of her pack and passed one to him. Their supply of snack food, too, would be gone within another week. Then what would they eat? Squirrel stew for breakfast? If only she could go back to the day of the train crash. If only...

"You have to stop doing that," Miles said.

"Doing what?"

"Blaming yourself for the ills of the world. *That way madness lies.*"

"Old Testament proverb?"

"Shakespeare. *King Lear.*"

They ate in silence. Tanda left the last bite of granola bar in the palm of her hand and held it out to Zeus who gingerly took it.

"Good dog," she said.

"Great dog," Miles agreed.

"So what's on your agenda today?"

"Checking on the folks who are detoxing. Most should be through the worst of it, or nearing that point."

"Integrating them into Alpine and teaching them to pull their own weight isn't going to be easy."

"But necessary." He repeated his earlier sentiment, "We'll figure it out."

It was a scene she would remember for many years. Miles looking at her and smiling with his quiet confidence. Zeus lying in the first rays of morning light. The taste of coffee on her tongue. Later it would seem to her that the morning of July 3rd, nearly one month from the date of the train crash, was when everything really changed.

Stan Makowski appeared around the corner of the square, pushing his horse to a full gallop. He pulled up beside them, but he didn't bother to dismount. "Groups are approaching from the east and the west."

Tanda and Miles were on their feet instantly.

"Armed?" she asked.

"From the looks of it, yes."

"How far out?"

"They've both stopped for unknown reasons. Approximately five miles outside of town."

She didn't bother to question him further. If Stan said there was trouble approaching, then there was trouble approaching. They had a plan for just such an eventuality, but she had no idea how effective it would be.

"We'll meet at the gazebo in thirty minutes."

Stan nodded once, turned the horse, and shot off in the opposite direction he'd come from.

"I'll get my medical supplies and meet you there."

"Bring your interns."

He started away, then strode back toward her. Putting a hand on each of her shoulders, he waited for her to look directly at him, to settle. "I'm not going to promise you everything will be fine. We're well past that. But we are in this together. You're not doing it alone, Tanda."

"Right."

"Thirty minutes."

"Yes."

He whistled once to Zeus and the two took off at a jog.

Tanda walked at a fast clip toward the police department. She found herself being grateful for the quiet of the morning she'd shared with Miles, for the simple food they'd eaten, for the people who would gather to protect the community of Alpine.

A silent alarm had been rung—one delivered from person to person. There was no banging of the drums, no clanging of the symbols. The enemy was at their gate, and she had no intention of giving away the fact that she was aware they were there.

By the time she jogged into the police department, Conor Johnson was standing in front of the equipment locker, pulling out rifles, handguns, and ammunition. "All of it?"

"All of it."

He didn't argue, and Tanda was grateful for that. They could hold a portion back for future attacks, but if they lost today what would be the point?

The station itself was surprisingly quiet, which meant that everyone was doing what they were supposed to do. Nearly everyone was gone.

"Body armor?" Conor asked.

"Yes." There wasn't enough of it, but they'd give it to the people on the front line.

The federal 1033 Program allowed the transfer of excess military equipment to police departments at no cost other than shipping to said departments. Alpine hadn't participated to the extent that some of the other departments had. Large metropolitan departments like Houston and El Paso had received everything from riot gear to tear gas to mine-resistant, ambush- protected vehicles.

Alpine had received extra ammunition, night vision goggles, and half a dozen assault rifles. That had been all they could ever envision needing, and still it had caused quite the stir. No one, least of all Tanda, wanted to think of the folks hired to protect a town using military-grade supplies against the citizens of that town.

But this was different.

The police would be fighting side by side with the citizens. They would be fighting for their very existence.

Edna locked her purse in the bottom drawer of her desk, checked the pistol she wore on her hip, and stood at the door, waiting.

Conor picked up two of the bags filled with supplies, Tanda picked up two more, and the three stepped out into what should have been a beautiful morning. It wasn't. Even the clouds building in the west seemed ominous. The wind had picked up, and the sound of a sign banging against a building carried to them.

They didn't speak. They didn't need to.

Edna locked the door, and they walked three abreast to the gazebo.

What Tanda saw when she turned the corner toward that park shouldn't have surprised her, but it did. Men, women, and teens were in small groups, checking their weapons, speaking quietly, waiting. She allowed her gaze to drift from group to group until she found Keme. Their eyes met and he nodded once. Lucy was by his side. Both had pistols on their hips, and Keme had brought his hunting rifle.

A hunting rifle.

This wasn't going to be easy.

She climbed the steps of the gazebo and her thoughts flashed back to the night the satellite fell. She remembered how fistfights had broken out and pandemonium had seemed so very close. But they'd pulled back from that edge. They'd assessed their situation, sought and found answers, and all that was left to do now was to see this day through.

In a voice meant for Tanda's ears only, Stan and Jorge delivered their reports. They'd been monitoring the east and west roadblocks. The approaching parties hadn't been seen by the men and women standing guard, but rather from the scouts that they sent out on irregularly timed circuits.

Next she turned to Logan.

"I've gathered up twenty extra horses," he said. "That was all I could get."

"We'll make it work." She tried to speak with a confidence she didn't quite feel.

He reached out, squeezed her arm, then turned back toward his group. They'd been through the plan for this situation many times.

Each person had their assigned position. She wanted Logan near her, but he was needed with Miles. A triage center would be set up at the train depot.

Clearing her throat, she turned toward the crowd. There was no use sugar-coating what was happening. Each man and woman needed to be fully aware of what they faced.

"We have a group of approximately fifty men and women positioned five miles west of town. They're hunkered down at the roadside park on Highway 90."

"Damn Marfa miscreants," muttered Gonzo, which earned a laugh from the crowd.

"We don't know they're from Marfa, though it's a fair assumption. What we do know is that they have at least a dozen vehicles."

That quieted everyone. They'd considered several scenarios, but the most likely one was that any attackers would be similarly equipped and walking or riding horses.

"We still have a few vehicles with gas," Jackson Castillo said. "They're yours if you want them."

"Thank you, but no. For one thing, we'd be heard. At this point, they may not know that we're aware of them. I'd like to keep it that way. Also," She stared around at the crowd that had grown to several hundred. "We can do this on foot and with the horses. We can save the vehicles and the fuel for the next emergency."

She was relieved to see several folks nod in agreement.

She raised her voice so she could be heard throughout the crowd. "Our bigger problem is to the east. There's a group of nearly one hundred at the junction of Old Marathon Road and Hwy 90.

We suspect that group will divide." Adrenaline began to pump through her veins. She had to breathe deeply to slow her heart rate because her mind was screaming for her to GO, DO SOMETHING, DO IT QUICK.

"I want Group 3 on the western edge. Don't go past the Hampton unless you hear from me. Stan..." She turned to find her friend and best officer. She pushed away the thought of his wife and children. She needed him, and Stan wouldn't even consider sitting this one out. "Choose half a dozen of your best riders and send them around so that they'll come up behind the group at the roadside park. Logan has extra horses if you need them. Clear?"

Stan nodded in the affirmative.

Tanda turned back to Jackson Castillo. "You'll take Groups 1 and 2 to the east. Group 1 will set up at the animal shelter on Old Marathon Road. Group 2 stays on 90 East, forward of the road block one mile, but no farther. If any of your people need a horse, they're to see Logan. Clear?"

"Clear."

"Group 4 stays in the center of downtown." Tanda hesitated as she scanned the crowd again, but she hadn't missed her. Regina Grant wasn't there. When was the last time she'd seen the woman? The day before? Two days before? She shook her head, pulled herself back to the issues at hand. "Conor will lead Group 4."

The younger man's head jerked up in surprise, but he didn't shy away from the responsibility. He nodded, crossed his arms, and Tanda knew that he could and would handle whatever came his way.

"Groups 1, 2, and 3 have runners. If people in Group 4 are needed, they'll be sent for, but Conor, don't deploy more than half of your people. If one of those attacking groups gets through, you're our final defense."

She stopped talking then and looked out at the crowd of people who she knew were willing to give their lives for their family, their friends, and their town. Pastor Tobias was standing in the middle of a group of teens. She saw old Mr. Avery, who had threatened Mrs. Benson's dog with his shotgun. Mrs. Crowder, who was nearing seventy, was checking her Glock. A month ago, Tanda would have been worried about Dylan Spencer, but any bravado the boy had once sported was gone. He had literally matured before her eyes and was now a valued member of the defensive team.

She saw Keme stepping closer to Lucy. Her brother and his wife had thought they could stay out of this, but in the end they'd stepped up to join their neighbors.

She didn't see Melinda Stone or Ben Cason. Of course she didn't. Melinda was dead and Ben was...he was missing.

The people who were left were a cohesive group, but they weren't a perfect one.

Some were too old. Others were too eager, and a few looked scared. She thought that might be a good thing.

"I hoped it wouldn't come to this, prayed it wouldn't. But it's here now. We can't..." She licked her lips and wished for a drink of water. "We can't change what has happened or what has brought us to this point, but we can...we will protect our lives in this place. It's all we have, folks. The government isn't showing up. We can't wait for anyone from Austin or DC to swoop in at the last minute."

"Keep Austin weird, and keep the politicians out of my town," Gonzo hollered, raising his hands above his head, which brought a cheer from ranchers and artists alike.

Tanda's mind insisted on flipping through memories of the last month—the train wreck, chasing Owen down and arresting him. The crashed satellite north of town. Sitting in the courtyard of the McDonald Observatory and hearing Felicia's story of tragedy and fear and death. Zeus alerting them to Quinton Cooper. The charred remains of their hospital. Holding Abuela's hand as she passed. Melinda Stone's body. Stan's newborn daughter. Keme and Lucy. Miles and Logan.

Miles Turner and Logan Wright.

She looked for and found the two men who had become her closest friends—standing together, watching her steadily, willing to do whatever was necessary.

Things could be worse.

She wasn't in this alone.

None of them were in this alone.

"Miles and Logan will be running the triage center at the train depot. As for the groups closing in on us, I expect their plan is to wait until darkness to attack. We'll bring it to them instead. We'll take the offense at exactly twelve noon." Tanda wished she had another hour, but she didn't. It was time to move, to get in position, to let each group leader come up with the best plan of attack. "You've come together, and I'm proud of you. Be careful.

Be as safe as you can be. No heroes—no unnecessary risks. You do your best to live to fight another day."

Chapter 24

M ILES AND LOGAN HAD been working on the triage center since their return from McDonald Observatory, when they'd found the charred remains of the town's medical center. On normal days—if any day since June 6th could be considered normal—patients came to his office in downtown Alpine. He also had interns, mostly students from Sul Ross, who conducted house calls for patients who weren't ambulatory.

A good portion of their planning dealt with those who currently required medical attention, but another significant part of their planning had been for this—for an attack where there would be casualties.

A centrally located triage center seemed like a necessary component of post-modern Alpine. Zeus tagged along beside Miles as he walked up and down the rows of cots. They had curtained off one end of the old train depot to serve as a physical examination and treatment area. There, he and Logan would work side by side. He wondered what his colleagues in Houston would think of him conducting medical triage with a veterinarian, and he decided he didn't care. Logan had a solid understanding of medicine, and he didn't panic in a tight spot—something he'd proven again and again.

Stationed near every third cot was a supply cart. Their lack of adequate supplies worried Miles more than any other aspect of what they were attempting to do. They were woefully short on everything from antibiotics to IV fluids. But they'd managed to cobble together what they had. They would use whatever was available until it ran out.

Floodlights that were powered by a generator also ran down the length of the room. Hopefully they wouldn't be needed. Hopefully this would be over well before dark, but it was better to have them and not need them, than need them and not have them.

A pharmacy of sorts was set up behind the ticket counter. Everything was sorted by type of medication and clearly labeled. Only Miles, Logan, or the nurses would be allowed to check out medication, and Anita Sanchez was in charge of maintaining the log for supplies. Having worked with her the last several weeks, having depended on her again and again, Miles was confident that nothing would get past Anita.

The station master's office had been converted into a staff break room—complete with chairs, two cots, and a table which held a twenty-gallon water jug, cups, several boxes of protein bars, and surgical gowns, gloves and masks. Though there was no running water, someone had installed a vertical water tank and converted the old faucet to a low-flow drip system. Where that had come from, Miles had no idea, but the system worked. It even included a pedal mechanism to turn the water on and off. Next to the sink was an industrial size pump bottle of hand soap. They could wash their hands and maintain at least a basic degree of sanitation as they went from patient to patient.

He walked to the station door. His interns were standing in small groups or sitting at the tables—twenty very young, somewhat frightened men and women. Sixteen of them were Sul Ross students. The other four—including Tanda's niece, Akule—had volunteered though they had no college credits in any related health field. All had proven to be quick learners. Since they had five nurses from the medical center, all capable and experienced, he'd broken the interns up into groups of four, with an RN supervising each group. The fifth RN had acted as a floater when someone else took a day off.

Everyone quieted as he stepped outside the station door. Logan, who had been meeting with the nurses, stood and walked over beside him.

"You're as prepared as you can be for this," Miles said. "I can assure you that whether you're doing your first round of emergency triage at MD Anderson Hospital in Houston or in a train station in Alpine Texas..."

That earned him a few smiles.

"It's going to be hard. You're going to see things that you'd rather not. You're going to be scared and wonder what you signed up for." Now every face was somber, some people staring at the ground, others with their eyes locked on Miles.

"Here's the thing though. Because you are here, we will save some. We might not save them all—prepare yourself for that. But we'll do our very best for your family and your neighbors."

He glanced at Logan, who cleared his throat and stepped forward. "Remember to fill out your Emergency triage notes. You'll want to skip that part. You'll tell yourself it's more important to move on to the next patient, but the forms are a critical step. After your patient moves through triage and into the care unit, that piece of paper will inform the next caregiver exactly what you've done. Without that information, we're just stumbling around in the dark. Any questions?"

There weren't.

They'd gone over this scenario more than once.

They were as prepared as they could be.

The adrenaline surge that Miles had been feeling didn't last. First one hour, then another passed with no word from either side of town.

"It'll be noon at least, probably later." Logan nodded toward one of the cots. "You could catch some sleep."

"There's not even a chance that I could manage to sleep." Miles appreciated the offer though. He knew what was ahead of them, could at least guess at the types of things they'd be dealing with. Still, there was nothing they could do other than wait. "Cards?"

"Sure."

So they sat in the break room, playing penny ante poker though neither had any change in their pockets.

The first patient arrived before the shooting started. The man had chest pains and trouble pulling in a deep breath, which was fairly easy to treat since Miles couldn't order any tests. It wasn't like they could perform a cardiac cath on the guy. Instead, Miles gave him nitroglycerin and handed him off to one of the interns with orders to make sure he was hydrated and check his vitals every thirty minutes.

He checked his watch. Ten minutes before noon. He walked to the breakroom, stared out the window, and prayed.

The wounded started arriving thirty minutes later. The first few weren't directly related to combat. Someone who had been stepped on by a horse. Another person had passed out, probably from heat exhaustion. And a third had suffered a rattlesnake bite. Fortunately, it hadn't been a direct bite or the man would probably have died.

They heard the occasional pop of gunfire, but the downtown area remained eerily quiet. Logan walked over to speak with Conor Johnson, who had taken over as the leader of Group 4 when Regina couldn't be found. Conor said they'd heard nothing. No runners had made it to town—which was either a very good or a very bad thing.

Their luck wouldn't hold.

With two groups attacking from opposite ends it couldn't possibly hold.

Everything changed twenty minutes later.

Their first battle-related injury was a gunshot to the thigh of one of their Sul Ross rodeo team members. He knew that because the kid kept saying, "A bull ride never hurt this bad."

He made sure the bullet had exited, cleaned the wound, applied a compress, and filled out the care form. Miles then handed him over to an intern with instructions to start him on antibiotics and keep him on the care side for at least three hours. The kid argued because he wanted to go right back to help, and Miles took that as a good sign that morale was high.

He cleaned up, donned new gloves and mask, then hurried back to the treatment room. Logan was performing CPR on a man whose abdomen had been torn up with spray from a shotgun. The man had no pulse and had lost an immense amount of blood. "Call it," he said before heading back to his side of the room. The intern's hand shook as she wrote the time of death on the care form.

They worked like that for over an hour, uncertain of what was happening on the edge of town, uncertain of whether they were winning or losing. But then again, could this possibly be what winning looked like?

As soon as a patient was whisked away by an intern, another took his place. Miles ripped off gloves and his surgical gown, donned another, and got back to work. He found a rhythm. He didn't second-guess himself. He worked efficiently and objectively until his intern wheeled in the next patient and he looked at the woman lying there.

She'd taken a bullet in the shoulder. She might have survived that, but someone had used a knife to slit open her abdomen. A well-intentioned runner had literally held her stomach together as they rushed toward triage. But there was nothing he could do. He understood that, and looking into her eyes, he knew that she understood it too.

"Tell Keme I love him."

"I will." His heart felt as if it were going to slam through his chest. His adrenaline was screaming for him to DO SOMETHI NG...get her in ER, STAT...call for a surgeon.

He couldn't do anything.

There was no ER.

There were no surgeons.

Miles couldn't believe this was happening. He couldn't believe that a year ago he would have been able to save this woman, and now all he could do was watch her die. "He knows you love him, but I will."

"Don't give up."

Miles nodded, his throat suddenly too tight for words.

"Stay with me."

"I will. I will." He ripped off his surgical gloves, held her hand between both of his and shut down the part of his brain that was telling him to move on to the next patient. This woman had given everything, and he would honor that. They weren't in an emergency room in Houston. They were in Alpine Texas, and she should not have died like this.

"Doctor. Doctor Turner. Doctor—"

He looked up at the intern who had been assisting. The girl's face was blanched of all color.

"I can't get a pulse."

He glanced around. Everyone in the room was watching him. How long had he been holding her hand?

Logan walked over, tears pooling in his eyes. He, too, looked devastated. He knelt next to the cot, touched her face, closed his eyes for a moment, then turned his gaze to Miles. "There was nothing you could do."

Miles nodded. "Right. Right." He laid her hand gently by her side and gave it one last squeeze.

The intern charted the time of death, then wheeled the cot out the other side—the side that they'd hoped they wouldn't need. There lying on the pavement where people should have been waiting to board a train to Del Rio or San Antonio were instead people who had been zipped into body bags.

He shook his head and raised his eyes to the sky. But there was nothing to see. No indication of whether they were winning or losing. Only the dark clouds that had blotted out the sun, promising rain that they had longed for, a storm that might provide water and life. As he watched, the first fat drops began to hit the ground.

Miles made his way back inside to his next patient.

Chapter 25

Regina turned to Ben Cason. "Take your men to the campus. Now."

"But—"

"Now, Ben. If anyone is standing guard, and I doubt there is, you can handle it. We need those supplies."

He looked doubtful, but he nodded once and took off at a jog.

She turned back toward the scene before her and raised her Steiner M750 binoculars. They had been at the top of her bug-out list. Taking them from the supply locker in the police department had been easy. Now they would give her an edge over Tanda—the binoculars, and her position, which was high on the hill outside of town. Tanda's attention was on her eastern and western flanks—as it should be. From her vantage point, Regina could see the teams scrambling into position.

But Ben would approach from the south on Highway 118. There was nothing between Alpine and Big Bend. It was the least likely direction for Tanda to cover. The plan was to go through the middle of town, to move quietly and quickly to the Sul Ross campus.

They would get in.

They would take the supplies they needed.

After all, their very existence depended on it.

She wished it hadn't come to this. She wished there had been another way, but if there was one thing she'd learned while working in a large city, it was to never shy away from an unpleasant decision.

Leaving Alpine had been easy. She'd known that she was never truly one of Tanda's precious team. She had never fit in. Her Houston days had followed her to Alpine, and that was fine with her. That experience in America's fourth-largest city had prepared her to win today.

The key was to not think of the people who obstructed their path as individuals. After all, they had the option to back away. If they chose to fight, they understood the risk.

It wasn't as if any of them had ever been her friend.

Chapter 26

MILES HAD HIS HANDS inside Jorge Rodriguez's abdomen when Conor Johnson burst into the room.

"Stay back," Miles barked.

Logan was helping him, holding back the skin and muscle with forceps so that Miles could get to the artery that had ruptured. Sweat slipped down his forehead, temporarily obscuring his vision. An intern moved closer, wiped his brow, and he nodded once.

"Just one more minute, Logan."

"Hang in there, Jorge." Logan kept his hands perfectly still, but his eyes were on the man they were trying to save. Could he hear them? Maybe. "Just hang on. You're not getting away from us that easy."

Miles pinched the vein, staunched the flow of blood, and quickly sewed it off. "Close him."

He stripped off his gloves and surgical gown, then walked over to Conor, whose eyes were frozen on the man lying on the cot.

"Is he going to make it?"

"If he doesn't die from infection or loss of blood, yes."

Conor shook his head once, then pulled his gaze back to Miles. "I wanted to ask your opinion on something."

"Let's step outside."

He motioned Conor toward the courtyard. They would have had more privacy on the platform side of the train station, but he didn't think Conor needed to see the bodies laid out there. They stood near the building, under the roof overhang as rain continued to fall steadily. Any other day and they would be celebrating the rainfall. They desperately needed it. Today, though, it was one more obstacle to overcome.

Conor took a big gulp of fresh air, then plunged in to describing his dilemma. "Half of my men were needed on the east side. Now a runner has shown up saying that someone is at Sul Ross. But Tanda said to leave the other half here in the middle of town. You know, in case..."

His voice trailed off, and Miles realized that standing before him was a twenty-something-year-old kid who had been saddled with a tremendous amount of responsibility.

"Probably it's nothing," Miles said.

Conor nodded, but he didn't look convinced.

"No one has breached the east or west side, or you would have heard."

"On the other hand, our winter supplies are there," Conor crossed then uncrossed his arms.

"Send four of your people to check it out."

"That makes sense. Thanks." He left as quickly as he had appeared.

"Problem?" Logan had finished with Jorge, an intern had moved him into the care unit, and Logan was now sewing up a head wound on yet another Sul Ross student.

"Yeah. Maybe."

Logan handed the needle and thread off to an intern and jerked his head outside. This time they went to the platform side. Miles' gaze kept sliding toward her body bag, which was zipped up tight, providing protection against the rain. How had it come to this? What were they doing? Where would it end?

Glancing around to make sure they were out of earshot of the others, Miles relayed what Conor had said.

"Could a third group be attacking?"

"Maybe, but...from where? The western group must be from Marfa. The eastern group from Marathon.

"Unless they're both from the same place and they split in order to attack us from both sides."

"Which would have been very hard to do, especially without being noticed." Miles tried to picture Alpine on his GPS map—a rather small dot in the west Texas desert. "Nothing's been reported from our spotters to the north, and going south on 118 there is nothing, no community at all until you reach the Rio Grande."

"Right." Logan rested his back against the wall of the train station. "I don't like it though. Look, it's not a coincidence that the eastern and western attacks are happening simultaneously."

"You think it's coordinated."

"A coincidence of that magnitude seems unlikely. It has to be."

"And if it's a coordinated attack, then maybe the purpose of that—"

"Is to keep everyone busy while they pillage our supplies."

If that was what was happening, Miles had just sent four people into a trap.

"Can you handle things here?"

"Yes. Go."

Miles turned to head back through the triage center when Logan called out to him. Reaching under his shirt, he removed a pistol from a hip holster, then pulled an extra magazine from his jeans pocket.

Miles accepted them both with a nod. It wasn't his first time to hold a gun, and he certainly wasn't adverse to protecting himself ...but as someone who sewed up gunshot wounds, he wasn't keen on inflicting the same.

Still—their supplies were critical.

How would they survive the winter without the food and medicine stored there?

Zeus had been waiting in the courtyard. As Miles jogged out of the building, the dog jumped up and matched his pace.

Who could be behind a very well-coordinated attack? Melinda Stone was dead—he'd been with Tanda when they'd found her body. Ben Cason didn't seem competent or proactive enough to coordinate such a thing, but it had to be someone from Alpine. How else would they have known the supplies were at the university?

Or was it simply a lucky guess on the thieves' part?

Miles tried to think positive. Perhaps they were dealing with a greedy bastard who had no idea how to use his weapon. Perhaps threatening the attacker would send him or her scurrying away like a desert rabbit.

He jogged through the rain, darting from building to building so he wouldn't be seen. But who was he hiding from? Their adversaries were on the outskirts of town—weren't they? He finally spotted Dixie Peters, Emmanuel Garcia, Gonzo, and a young woman he didn't know—all hunkered down at the corner of the Admin building.

He whistled once—a short, sharp sound—hoping Dixie wouldn't turn and shoot him. She glanced his direction, nodded, and touched Gonzo on the shoulder. All four turned to watch his approach.

"Thought you were helping on our western flank."

Dixie smiled grimly as she checked her weapon. "Brought in some wounded, dropped them off with your interns, then decided to check in on Conor."

"She couldn't resist the opportunity to catch whoever might be behind this," Emmanuel explained.

"So we think this is coordinated?"

"It would seem to be." This from Gonzo, who ran his fingers through his beard and grinned. "But if they thought they could sneak past us, they're in for a surprise."

The university appeared deserted other than their small group. The administration building was located in the center of the campus. They were on the courtyard side. The other side of the building faced a parking area, but you had to go through the campus to get there. It had seemed like the best place to store everything. You'd have to pass anyone living on campus in order to reach the supplies—and a more obvious place would have been the sports center, which is why they hadn't chosen it. The admin building was full of offices with very little open space—it seemed a safe bet that it would be the last place anyone would look.

So how did these people know where the supplies were? "How big a group are we talking about?"

"Four people in a panel van," Dixie said.

"How did we not hear it?"

"Electric."

Wow. That meant someone had used what precious generator power they had to charge a vehicle.

Emmanuel swiped a hand over his face. They were crowded under the roof overhang. The rain had picked up and they were all drenched. The temperature had dropped with the rain, but the day still felt oppressive. Zeus flopped to the ground, panting as his gaze remained fixed on Miles.

"It gets worse," Gonzo said. "We were able to make out one of them. Ben Cason."

So he wasn't dead. Had he killed Melinda Stone? Miles didn't think so. He thought that someone like Ben Cason would be following orders. The question was, who was the person giving the orders?

"They've been stashing our supplies in their van for the past fifteen minutes or so." This from the young woman who Miles realized he did know. She'd been a barista at the coffee shop in town. He sent her a weak smile which she returned.

"Do we have a plan?"

"Yeah." Dixie's voice was a low growl. Even Zeus noticed it and responded by putting his head down on his paws and whining. "Our plan is to stop them."

"We could send someone to fetch Conor. Wait for reinforcements."

Dixie shook her head. "I don't think we have time for that."

As they watched, the three men doing the heavy lifting pushed a dolly toward the back of the van and began unloading their supplies. Ben stood guard, holding an M-16 rifle rather awkwardly.

Dixie turned back toward them and motioned for their group to back away from the corner of the building. There was little risk they could be heard over the rain and thunder, but why take the chance? Once they'd moved a few feet away, she said, "This is what we're going to do..."

Dixie's plan made sense. Her job as fire chief had taught her to quickly and accurately assess a situation. They would split and approach from opposite ends, and they'd wait for her signal. Once the three men were back inside the building, they'd disarm Ben. The others were probably carrying firearms, but they'd be focused on the supplies. By the time they could drop what they were carrying and pull their weapons, they'd be surrounded.

If everything went as it should.

They moved into position. The thieves went back inside, and Ben stood staring out toward the parking area—apparently convinced that if trouble came it would come from that direction.

Miles moved into position at the back of the van. Gonzo slipped behind Ben with the agility of a man half his age. Miles could just make out the sound of a pistol's hammer being cocked.

"Give me the weapon, Ben. Even I can't miss a shot to the back of your head at point blank range."

Dixie was there to accept the weapon.

"I can explain—" His voice shook, and his eyes darted back and forth between the building and the group surrounding him.

"No. You can't. Say anything else, and Gonzo will shut you up permanently."

Ben didn't argue with that.

Miles thought he heard the three retreating. He dared to peek around the corner of the van and saw no one. Good. So far, so good.

Which left Miles, Zeus, Emmanuel, and the barista—whose name was Kelly—in the back of the van.

The van was three quarters full with their supplies.

Miles stood inside the door of the van, his back pressed against its side. Zeus and Kelly were stationed closer toward the cab, where they'd wiggled some boxes forward and created a hidey-hole. Emmanuel was directly across from Miles.

They heard the approach of Ben's cohorts before they saw them.

Miles and Emmanuel stepped forward at exactly the same moment, their weapons raised and locked on the men.

"Don't move your hands," Emmanuel cautioned.

One fellow did. He dropped his box and went for his pistol. Emmanuel shot him as the box clattered to the ground. The other two men dropped their boxes and took off running.

Miles whistled. Zeus flew from the van and tackled the young man on the right, who lay on the ground, his head covered with his hands, screaming, "Get him off me. Just get him off." Kelly had catapulted from the van and landed on the guy who went left. He screamed in pain. Miles suspected from the awkward way he'd landed on his arm that he'd broken it.

"Great jump," Miles said as he helped Kelly up. "Where did you learn that?"

"High school track. Set the long jump record and it still hasn't been broken."

He high-fived her though it felt ridiculously carefree and absurd to do so. It also felt right. Adrenaline was pumping through his veins, and his heart rate was definitely accelerated. Who knew combat could be so satisfying?

Dixie and Gonzo returned with Ben, who now had his hands duct-taped behind his back.

"You don't want to do this," Ben said. "We were going to take the stuff and leave. We weren't going to hurt anyone."

He paled when he glanced down at the guy Emmanuel had shot. It was obvious the man was dead. Miles didn't need to check his pulse. The growing puddle of red was proof enough.

"You shouldn't have done that," Ben whispered.

"And you shouldn't have tried to steal our supplies." Dixie's voice was filled with barely contained rage. "How could you do this, Ben? People would have died if you'd managed to get away with this—people you know and used to work for. People who were your friends and neighbors."

"People have already died," he practically spat at her. "Don't act like you care—maybe for the people who fall in line with your agenda, but no one else. You didn't care about me. You didn't care about me or Melinda or Regina."

Regina Grant, one of Tanda's officers, was behind this? Miles barely knew her, but still it was hard to fathom. How could someone who'd been on the right side of things suddenly go over to the wrong side? Why? What motivation could possibly be strong enough?

"So Regina's behind this." Dixie shook her head. "Of course she is. She was here when we decided to use this place. She created a diversion at the east and west end for this very reason. So you could drive through the middle of town and take what isn't yours."

"Why do you get to make the rules?" Ben countered. "Why do you always think you're right? You people, you're always convinced you're right."

"Did Regina kill Melinda Stone?"

"Stone got greedy. Regina did what she had to do."

"Duct-taped and then murdered a woman? She had to do that?"

"Yes, she did. Don't act like you wouldn't have done the same thing."

In frustration, Dixie pulled the roll of duct tape from her back pack, ripped off a piece and slapped it over his mouth. While they'd been talking to Ben, Gonzo had duct-taped the other two. The one with a broken arm was openly weeping, and Miles felt a moment of sympathy for the kid. He probably wasn't old enough to legally drink, but he'd put himself in league with people who were capable of unconscionable violence, unprovoked violence.

"Gonzo, Kelly, and Emmanuel, take them to the jail." Dixie sounded tired. That would be the adrenaline slowing. Her shoulders slumped, and she stared at the dead guy on the ground.

"I'll come by the jail and set his arm as soon as I can," Miles said to Dixie as they stood there, watching the thieves be escorted back to town through the pouring rain. He glanced at Dixie then down at the dead guy. "Do you know him?"

"No."

"I'll send two of my interns over to take care of him. We can put the supplies back inside when this is over."

"What if it isn't over?" The rain had turned to a downpour. Dixie didn't bother to wipe her face. She stood there, staring at him with a look that was so desperate, so devoid of hope, that Miles felt his heart ache for her. "What if it just goes on and on?"

He took her by the shoulders then and waited until she looked at him. "You know what this feeling is. Your adrenal glands are spent, and your cortisol is all used up."

She crossed her arms, hugged herself, but she didn't speak. She didn't agree with him or argue with him.

"This is exhaustion, Dixie. Nothing more. You've experienced it before, probably after every fire you've ever fought. Don't give in to it."

"Right." She nodded once with little conviction, and then again. "You're right."

He hoped that he was.

Miles thought of the bodies laid out on the train station's platform. He thought of her body. They might win this particular battle, they just might, but oh, what a price they had paid.

The rain continued—rain that would fill the cisterns, water the crops, make life possible. He walked beside Dixie, each lost in their own thoughts. When they reached the train station, Dixie reach out and squeezed his arm. "Thanks, Miles. For everything." Then she continued on to check in with Conor.

Activity at the triage center had calmed. "No new casualties since you left," Logan said. "What happened at the university?"

Miles caught him up.

"I didn't know Regina well," Logan admitted. "But I'm still surprised. It's always hard to understand someone who holds an opposing view."

"Her opposing view has resulted in a lot of death."

"True, but if it hadn't been her leading them it would have been someone else." Logan snapped on a fresh pair of gloves. "This battle...it was inevitable."

He moved into the care area to check on his patients.

Miles heard the clatter of horse hooves on pavement, something that would have sounded completely bizarre a month before. He stepped outside to see who it was, and there riding toward him in the downpour was Tanda.

He had delivered a lot of bad news in his time as a doctor. He had dealt with death too many times. His mind brushed up against the memory of his wife and daughter. He missed them so much that it was a physical pain in his chest, and yet...a part of him was also thankful that they hadn't lived to face this.

Tanda handed Roxy's lead to Stan.

"What is it?"

He thought of the supplies, of Ben Cason and Regina Grant. Of Rodriguez in the care room, fighting for his life. But that wasn't what she was asking. He knew her well enough to understand that she'd want the news immediately. There was no point in trying to soften it, and he respected her too much to avoid the question.

"Lucy."

And for a moment, the fight went out of Tanda Lopez. All color drained from her face, her shoulders fell and her breath caught in her chest. For a moment, she lingered between understanding and needing to shy away from the truth.

Understanding won.

"Where is she?" The words were a whisper, a cry for mercy.

He walked her through the triage center, which was blessedly empty, though the signs of the battle they'd fought there were everywhere. Bloody scrubs in the large trash can—sponges and forceps, suture kits and scalpels and IV solution. They walked past it all to the train station platform where passengers were supposed to wait.

The bodies were lined out in a row—a total of nineteen in all. He didn't have to check the name tags. He walked her over to Lucy's and knelt with Tanda as she unzipped the bag. Tears fell from her eyes, a baptism of love. She sat there a moment, cradling Lucy's face in her hands, her lips moving silently in prayer or confession or a final goodbye.

Then she leaned forward and kissed Lucy's forehead.

Without another word, she stood and walked away.

Miles rezipped the bag, then turned and watched Tanda go—a slight figure, momentarily diminished by the burden of leadership she carried. The burden of love. Tanda Lopez had led them through a crisis no one could have imagined. She was—physically, emotionally, even spiritually—one of the strongest people he had ever met. And he believed, he had to believe, that she would overcome this latest loss as she had the others.

He didn't realize at first that she was walking toward someone. Then a figure on a horse appeared. The rider approached her and dismounted. Both stood, for a moment, the rain nearly obscuring his view of them. When the man stepped closer, Miles thought that it might be Keme. He knew for certain when the man collapsed to the ground and Tanda knelt beside him.

She knelt in the rain and the mud, put her arms around him, and held on. She literally covered her brother's body with her own.

Chapter 27

THEY MARKED THE ONE-MONTH anniversary of the crash by honoring their dead. The bodies were laid side by side in the Alpine cemetery. They weren't the first to die since the crash, but they were the first to give up their lives defending their neighbors, their family, and their town.

Pastor Tobias read the 23rd Psalm.

Edna sang *Amazing Grace*.

Tanda stood with her mother and father on her left, Keme and Akule on her right. Her niece had said little since the Battle for Alpine, as it had come to be known. Tanda understood that she was processing all that had happened—the loss of so many dreams, some friends, and her mother.

Keme stepped forward to speak.

She wasn't sure what she expected him to say or do. Perhaps she'd thought that he would wave his rain stick or perform one of the dance rituals he had been taught by their grandparents.

As he often did, Keme surprised her.

His voice was strong and clear, full of the grief and the hope that held them all together.

"As many of you know, my wife loved poetry. If you spent even five minutes with her while she enjoyed a glass of wine, then I suspect you were made to suffer through quotes from some of her favorite poets."

A light, poignant laughter whispered through the crowd.

"I teased her a lot about that, but now...now it seems to me that if there was ever a time when we needed the beauty and hope that comes from poetry, today is that day." Keme didn't brush at the tears coursing down his cheeks. He let them fall, let his gaze take in all of the people gathered together before glancing down at the slip of paper in his hand. "It seems appropriate to share another of her favorites, a passage from *Ulysses* by Alfred Tennyson."

The crowd quieted, stilled completely.

> *"Though much is taken, much abides; and though*
> *We are not now that strength which in old days*
> *Moved earth and heaven,*
> *That which we are, we are—"*

He looked up then, sought and found Tanda's eyes, let his gaze linger upon his daughter and his parents, closed his eyes for a moment and pulled in a deep breath.

> *"That which we are, we are—*
> *One equal temper of heroic hearts,*
> *Made weak by time and fate, but strong in will*
> *To strive, to seek, to find, and not to yield."*

Silence followed Keme's reading, and then another person stepped forward to speak followed by another. Tanda couldn't have testified to who they were or what they said. Her mind had snagged on the last two lines Keme had quoted.

> *"Made weak by time and fate, but strong in will*
> *To strive, to seek, to find, and not to yield."*

Was that what they had become?

Characters in Homer's *Odyssey*?

She could remember struggling with both Tennyson and Homer in her high school senior English class, and now, finally, she understood what they had been trying to say. She understood what it meant *to strive, to seek, to find, and not to yield*.

Tanda looked across the mourners gathered, and it was literally everyone left in Alpine other than the infirm, those caring for them, or the men and women who were on patrol. This was their town. Less than half the size it had been a month before.

That which we are, we are—

The potluck which followed reminded Tanda of the earlier one when they'd met to eat what was about to spoil. The food didn't resemble that day at all—now the tables were filled with rabbit stew and fried venison and precious vegetables grown from their gardens.

There were no sodas, no beer or wine of any kind, only water—and they were grateful for it. Where before they'd eaten from their abundance, now they shared from their scarcity.

But the children still dashed between the tables, chasing a ball or a cat or one another. Teenagers sat in groups, listening and talking. No one stared at a phone's screen. No one checked social media or watched a video. Stan and Zoey sat with their four children, including tiny Chloe, the first new life born after the crash. There would be more. Children who would grow up in a world their parents had been unwilling to imagine and unable to prevent.

And yet, was it in fact worse than what they had before? Of course it was. One part of her mind knew and accepted that. They had little medicine, inadequate food supplies and no communication. And yet...

Artists sat beside ranchers.

Black beside white beside brown.

Teens with the elderly.

The measure of a person was no longer whether he or she shared your political opinions or your definition of what a couple should be or even your ideas of social justice. It seemed to Tanda that the measure of a person had become what it should have been all along. *Will you fight beside me? Will you share what you have? Will you receive what I have to share?* They had cobbled together their own version of a community.

One month earlier, she had sat here with Logan and Miles. They'd been so full of questions and energy. So intent on confronting whatever lay ahead, so dead set on running toward their problems. That day was when they'd first decided to go to the observatory, to find out what they were facing. Now they knew, and Tanda had some understanding of what would need to be done.

Too many were missing from this gathering.

Too many had been lost.

And yet...Keme's and Tennyson's words whispered in her ear. *Though much is taken, much abides.*

Their family was not the only one which had suffered loss. It seemed to Tanda that no family remained unscathed. Perhaps it was their losses which would bind them together.

Miles and Logan waited until her family had finished their meal and moved away to speak with others. They gave her the space she needed to come to terms with all that had happened. And then, when enough time had passed, they sat down opposite her.

Logan offered a slight smile.

Miles watched her with his steady blue eyes.

It was amusing to see them sitting there like two brothers, two good friends who seemed to have known each other for their entire lives. And perhaps they had. Perhaps, in some way, they had.

"Miles and I thought we'd take a ride."

"We thought you might want to go along."

"Thought we'd at least ask."

She sat back, her plate of food largely untasted.

Glancing to the right, she saw Dylan standing at the edge of those assembled, holding the leads of three horses, including Roxy.

And suddenly riding was exactly what Tanda wanted to do, what she needed to do.

Together the three walked to the horses, Zeus ever close to Miles' side, and Tanda's mind was filled with the memory of the first time she'd seen the two of them walking down the streets of Alpine, walking toward her office.

"Stay with Dylan," Miles said softly. The dog sat obediently, head cocked to the side as if unsure why he was being left.

Dylan handed off the leads, then scratched Zeus behind the ear. "Come on, boy. Let's get you a venison bone."

Which was all the encouragement Zeus needed.

They rode in silence. The day was again warm, as it had been when she'd first ridden to Old Ranch Road with Stan, ridden to plead with a man she didn't know to come down from his cabin retreat and tend to their people.

They ascended the caliche road. Roxy moved easily along the path. Tanda wondered at how comfortable she felt on the horse, how natural this life had become now that it had been so abruptly forced upon them.

Halfway up, they stopped and turned back, looked toward the train wreckage that remained where it had landed. She supposed it would remain there for many years to come. The last of the afternoon's sun bounced off the train cars, spread across the land.

There wasn't a single moving vehicle to be seen in any direction—just the high Alpine desert as far as she could see, and beyond that the outline of the mountains. It was a good place, she realized. If you had to be anywhere during such a time as this, Alpine was a good place to be.

She glanced to her right and her left, tried to resist the smile tugging at her lips. It seemed sacrilegious to smile on a day commemorating so much grief, and yet...and yet, Lucy would insist on it. *Abuela* would nod her head in approval.

Neither Logan nor Miles nor Tanda could predict what new challenges they would face in the days to come. The one thing she knew, with absolute certainty, was that they would face whatever was coming together.

The End

*F*ROM *VEIL OF Confusion*
A Kessler Effect Novel, Book Two

They were up well before the sun. The items they would take with them had been laid out, catalogued, packed, and then sifted through again and repacked. What could be left? What would they need?

Winter items on the bottom.

Food near the top.

Weapons in their pockets.

They'd prepared the night before and the night before that. Harper didn't think they'd be able to sleep their last night in the old bus. She had thought they'd lie awake staring at the ceiling, imagining all that could go wrong. But she and Cade had both fallen immediately into the place of dreams and memories and hope.

They woke early. They always woke early, before the wild dogs had begun their foraging. There was little more to do than slip into their clothes and wait for the moment to shoulder their packs.

Cade had lit the single lantern and turned it to low. Harper drank in his profile—his strong jawline, warm brown eyes, slightly crooked nose. The nose helped him to fit into their world. No one should have movie-star looks, and Cade's nose saved him from that. But it was his hands that caused a lump to rise in her throat. It was his hands that were scarred, strong, capable, tender.

"We should eat something." He pulled out a piece of the hard bread they'd cooked in the campfire using a Dutch oven the day before, broke it in half, and handed it to her. "Would you like some butter with that?"

"And jam. Strawberry please."

Neither smiled at the old joke. It had passed between them so many times that now it felt like sand slipping through their fingers.

Harper continued watching Cade as she attempted to chew the tack. Studying him, it seemed she could trace the path of their lives since June 6th. His arms had grown stronger and tan, and his hair long. The beard came in thick with a bit of gray—something that had surprised them both. His shoulders seemed broader to her, though she supposed that was impossible. One's physique didn't change because of the burdens you were forced to carry.

And yet they had changed—irrevocably.

Those first weeks of June weren't something she cared to dwell on. The violence and terror and swiftness with which they'd descended into lawlessness. If she thought on those things, she was filled with a despair that threatened to strangle her.

Instead, she tried to call to mind the man she'd fallen in love with three months earlier and found she couldn't. The face she stared at now was the only one she knew. It showed his abiding love for her, his concern for what they were about to attempt, and the strain of a life lived in El Paso's northern barrio—otherwise known as *Lugar de Los Muertos*, or *Muertos Norte* for short.

Harper preferred northern barrio.

Cade pulled out his canister of filtered water, unscrewed the top, and passed it to her. The water was cold and a little gritty. The filters didn't catch everything, but if the water was going to kill her it probably would have done so by now. Harper drank her fill, passed it back to Cade, and watched as he guzzled the rest.

Then he stood and refilled it from the collection tank. A pipe fitted into the ceiling of the bus collected rain water, which in far west Texas was precious little. The water slid through the pipe, passed the two sets of filters, and settled into the collection tank, which was actually an old galvanized stock tank. Cade had walked an entire day looking for that tank. He'd searched a dozen abandoned farms on the outskirts of town.

His water purification system was just one reason the bus would be claimed before they'd reached the edge of the barrio.

Harper peeked through a slit in the blackout curtains. A crescent moon dipped toward the horizon. She watched until she was able to see the outline of the Franklin Mountains, then nodded to

Cade, and he doused the light. They left the bus more silently than the sun approached the horizon. They walked west.

Tía lived in a former FEMA trailer. The words were emblazoned on the side, though they'd faded in the harsh Texas sun. Harper didn't know how old Tíawas but would have guessed her to be in her eighties. She also didn't know if the woman was Hispanic or Native American, though ethnicities had ceased to matter long ago. She didn't even know if Tía had once had children or grandchildren. She lived alone and spoke only rarely of her life before.

Everyone called her Tía, and if there was a leader in the northern barrio, she was it.

No one entered the barrio without her approval.

No one dared to leave it without her blessing.

The rumors surrounding Tía were as numerous and varied as cacti in the desert. She'd healed a boy. She'd raised a woman from the dead. Her entire family had been killed in the fall. She'd always lived alone. She was a prophet or an empath or possibly a former spy.

Tía was sitting on the porch of her trailer, stroking an old tabby cat. How she managed to feed herself, let alone the cat, was a mystery. Harper suspected people dropped off a portion of what little they had, like sacrifices left on the steps of the Greek gods in hopes of finding favor.

"Cade and Harper, it is good to see you."

Cade threw a glance at Harper. Tía had been blind for at least as long as she'd lived in the northern barrio. How she knew it was them was yet another mystery. Perhaps the loss of her sight had sharpened her other senses. It was possible that they walked differently or smelled differently.

"What you have to tell me is best said inside." She gently set the cat on the ground, then pushed to her feet and led them into the single room that was her home.

One long wall of the trailer was fitted with shelves, and on those shelves sat hundreds of jars. Anyone who found a jar unshattered brought it to Tía. In turn, she filled them with herbs that she grew in the small plot of ground beside her trailer. That plot of ground was probably better guarded than the entire barrio. People depended on Tía's herbs for medical problems, emotional problems, even spiritual problems. Harper didn't know where the seeds had come from or how, given her blindness, Tía was able to tell one jar from another.

Once inside, Tía sat in the rocker and the cat jumped back onto her lap. "So, you're leaving?"

"Yes." Cade perched on the edge of the couch and Harper did the same. "We wanted to say goodbye and to thank you...for everything."

"You both have served an important role in our little community. The barrio will miss you, but your destiny does not lie here."

Harper let out a breath. She hadn't realized, until that moment, how much Tía's blessing meant to her.

"Which direction will you go?"

"North, through the Franklin Mountains." Cade stared at his hands. "We know to stay away from major roads."

Tía nodded and set the chair to rocking, studying the cat as her hand brushed it from head to tail, head to tail. Finally, she raised her head and offered a smile. Harper thought it was one of the most beautiful things she'd seen in a very long while—Tía's smiling face, lined with the wrinkles of fate and time, her dark skin weathered to the texture of soft leather, still-mostly-black hair braided and pulled over her left shoulder.

"I am sure you have given this considerable thought. No doubt you are as prepared as two *viajeros* can be." She again stroked the cat. "But you should go east, not north."

"East?" Harper's voice broke on the word. "There's nothing...east."

"Exactly. You will travel un-accosted."

"I don't understand." Cade laced his fingers together, elbows propped on his knees, and leaned forward. "We need to go north. How will going east—"

Tía held up a weathered hand. "The Guadalupe Mountains are full of caves, springs, even old cabins. The Mescalero Apache lived there for many years, and after that the white men came, looking first for water and later for oil."

"McKittrick Canyon." Cade scrubbed a hand over his face. "I've been there once, but, Tía..." The next words were offered gently, nearly a plea. "We need to go north."

"Climb the mountains to the east. You have your spy glass, yes?"

Cade hesitated, glanced at Harper, and finally nodded. Harper wondered again how the old blind woman could be aware of their silent communication, because Tía waited for that nod, then continued.

"You will be able to see a great distance in every direction from Guadalupe Peak. Possibly you will even see your future. And if there is danger and destruction, as you fear, you will see that too."

Cade looked to Harper then and waited for her response. Harper didn't know Tía's history or what gifts she actually possessed, but she was certain that her words had the ring of truth to them. She nodded once, and it was decided. They would abandon the route they'd so carefully planned. Instead, they would walk east.

Veil of Confusion, available on Amazon.

Author's Note

This book is dedicated to my sister, Pam, who loves a good dystopian read. Thanks for encouraging me to step back into the genre.

It's also dedicated to Heather Blodgett—my friend and dog-sitter extraordinaire. You help to keep me sane.

I visited and thoroughly researched Alpine, Texas and the surrounding locations mentioned in this book. Any changes made within the pages of this book were done so in order to expedite the plot of the book. In 1978, NASA scientist Donald J. Kessler published a paper titled, "Collision Frequency of Artificial Satellites: The Creation of a Debris Belt." This paper described a cascading collision of lower orbital satellites, something that has since been termed the Kessler Effect or the Kessler Syndrome. I have done my best to adequately present his theories within the text of this story. Any errors made in that representation are my own.

Many people were helpful in the writing of this book, including Kristy Kreymer, Tracy Luscombe, Judith Ann Oliver McGhee, and Matt Walter.

Teresa Lynn, I owe you a huge debt for your editing efforts on my behalf.

Joyce and Bruce, you are always an inspiration.

And, of course, Bob—I love you, babe.

 Vannetta Chapman is the USA Today and Publishers Weekly bestselling author of over 40 books in a variety of genres that include dystopian, suspense, romantic suspense, romance, and cozy mystery. She was an English teacher at the high school and collegiate level for fifteen years. She currently resides in the Texas Hill Country where she writes full times. For more information, visit her at her website www.Vannetta Chapman.com

Also by Vannetta Chapman

Veil of Mystery, A Kessler Effect Prequel
Veil of Anarchy, A Kessler Effect Novel, Book 1
Veil of Confusion, A Kessler Effect Novel, Book 2

Defending America Series
Coyote's Revenge, Book 1
Roswell's Secret, Book 2

Standalone Novel
Security Breach

See a complete booklist at www.VannettaChapman.com